Erotica for the Soul

Statistics show that most women are not seeking explicit scenes of sexual activity but rather character driven stories of romantic relationships that involve sex. RawrWoman provides the perfect venue for this exploration.

Erotica for the Soul
Vol. 1

By RawrWoman

Published by Peter Hansen

Most of the material in this book is excerpted from the RawrWoman.com free Website.
RawrWoman™

™REGISTERED TRADEMARK – MARCA REGISTRADA

Published by Peter Hansen
Cover design: Aziz & Jimy2014
Editing: Susan Kelejian and Peter Hansen

ISBN 978-0-9962312-9-9

~

INTRODUCTION

The short stories in "Erotica for the Soul" can be a new beginning for some; for those more adventurous and experienced in this genre it can be an excellent addition to your existing erotic literature library.

Our goal is to appeal to the female audience's senses. To create a place where you can find self-expression through the stories we devise, and let your inhibitions go.

Who is RawrWoman? Though RawrWoman is written mostly by and for a female audience, it was conceptualized and manifested by Peter Hansen, one of those rare males who understand the sophisticated nature of the female psyche. His initial goal was to create a unique niche between polite society and the billion-dollar xxx industry. In addition, he is focusing on an arousing destination built with the woman in mind, a place for women to feel safe, while focusing on the desire for a multi-layered stimulating experience.

Peter acknowledges the fact that women have been suppressed by means of exploitation, lack of validation and the different gender specific needs when it comes to sexual fantasy and exploration.
By creating RawrWoman, it is important that Peter invited a community of women to support and create together, which he has provided for by the launch of the website and by publishing female authored erotic literature.

We create content that entice, fascinate, and above all provide pleasure to the woman who indulges in all we have to offer.

Foreword

By Susan Kelejian

We females can be somewhat "complicated."
It's perfectly fine to be this way; we just need to
acknowledge who we truly are so we can return to
our sacredness of being in what I call, *"the authentic
feminine."* This definition, in my lexicon, includes
sexuality.

Expressed sexuality can be with a partner(s), or with
oneself. By saying we can be complex in our nature,
we tend to be sensual and sexual, and enjoy
ourselves in an immersion of all senses. Women, in
general, are less attracted to look at straight
pornography and more prone to reading descriptive
stories. That's one of the reasons why I love well-
written erotic literature.

Erotic literature can be a combination of fictional and
factional stories that are intended for arousal.
Through explicit language and that tell stories of
fantasy, it can be a safe exploration of our
imaginations, and something that we may never act
upon or in *reality* want to happen to us. For example,
one of the top erotic scenarios for women is to be
overpowered and raped. While this is a perfectly
acceptable *fantasy* since our imaginations will
control the situation, it does not mean in any
circumstance that we desire that in real life.

When language flourishes, erotic tales swerve and
soar in and out of our bodies, allowing emotions to
circle back into the here and now, with physiological
connections of pulses, heartbeats, and sensations.

In popular psychology magazines, it was stated that women who read romance and erotica novels have sex with their partners over seventy percent more often than women who don't, and that women who fantasize frequently have sex more often, have more fun in bed, and engage in a wider variety of erotic activities.

What are the shades of excitement that push the boundaries of the blurred inner lines between perversion and playfulness? Erotic literature is a difficult genre because of the nature of the beast itself we all come from such varied perspectives that what titillates the imagination is often on an individual basis. Conversely, there are themes that women have particularly found to be enticing, some that dance on the shadow side of our souls, others that are light and whimsical.

Erotic literature is nothing new: it has been around since...well, since people could write on papyrus. Poems in verse, lyrics, and short stories have survived since Ancient Greece. The Greeks believed that literature was both psychologically and spiritually important, making the sign above their library doors that read "a healing place for the soul" commonplace. After the printing press was established, censorship came into play because stories of erotica circulated at a much higher publication to the masses.

Arguably, one of the top female, if not *the* top female authors in erotic literature is Anais Nin, who broke the mold on how previously pornographic novels and short stories were penned. Coming out of the post-modernism surrealism movement and being able to utilize her writing strengths as part poetic, lyrical, magical realism, expressionistic, and one who wrote with a clear attention to emotions, thoughts, and psychological insights (particularly of women), Nin's work in "Delta of Venus" and "Little Birds" can be synonymous with women's erotica.

Noted as the foremost literary genius of our time, William Shakespeare wrote en explicit erotic poem of Venus and Adonis (where he compares the lovers as horses) and the Rape of Lucrece. Censorship often gives society a focus on the subject as taboo and therefore creates an often unwanted backlash of even more interest than if there wasn't any censorship to begin with. It makes it half the fun of "being bad and getting away with it" which can be itself a turn on.

Reading erotic literature can be somewhere in the middle of societal taboo and personal excitement as we find ourselves peeking into a world that's seductive and tantalizing.

What else comprises the authentic feminine? Part of this actualization is being able to use your voice without shame, blame, or guilt. Just by speaking aloud explicit words can be empowering. As a relationship therapist, I have found that a large percentage of adult woman have a hard time saying the name of their body parts, especially the vagina, cervix, lips etc. It sounds clinical, like something the *doctor* says. Women can feel embarrassed talking about it, discussing it, exploring it, where they like to be touched specifically etc. So how are we supposed to translate that to our partners and ask for our needs if we can't even talk about ourselves in that way? Using erotic literature will allow us to slowly slide into the sensual world without feeling silly, or guilty.

We don't need to deny the fact that we women are indeed, quite sexual. However, it's true that women can and do approach and engage in sex differently than men. We like to feel, to experience, to have a connection of our heart/mind/and body. We need to feel safe before we can really explore, openly and fully. We also like to have fun, be adventurous and role-play. There are some women who can completely compartmentalize between love and sex, but not many, as we find that it is often intertwined.

So, enjoy. Treat this like a delicious yet exotically flavored cake that has all the taste and none of the calories, carbs, or sugars. It is exceptionally tasty and yet won't do you any harm. Even if this sounds too good to be true, I bet you would want to try a slice. Bon Appetite!

Susan Kelejian lives in California with a slew of animals and one brilliant child. In addition to being a professional writer, she is an avid equestrian, mental health professional, theatre artist and educator. She loves word play, swordplay, and horseplay almost as much as foreplay. She's thrilled to be contributing to RawrWoman and working with Peter, especially in the area of helping to facilitate women's empowerment through steamy, sensual and sexually charged literature.

Erotica For the Soul
Vol. 1

TABLE OF CONTENTS

Included is 3 Personalized Erotic Love Letters, and a "How to Guide" you can use when you read and record it in your own voice, and get the full immersion experience with your lover...

~

Author: Elizabeth Cane
Elizabeth Cane has never been one to shy away from passion and adventure, whether it's exploring with a younger guy or pressing boundaries. She enjoys sharing some of her experiences, as well as adventures that come from where her mind wanders when left to her own devices.

"Elevator Fantasy"
By, Elizabeth Cane

For as long as I could remember, I've had a fantasy about encountering a handsome stranger in an elevator.

One night, my boss invited me to share some wine to celebrate a new client. We finished off an expensive bottle of Chateau Montelena Estate and he gingerly placed his hand on my knee. Feeling bold from the drink and taking a big chance, I whispered in his ear, detailing my fantasy. We knew we were heading to dangerous territory after sharing a steamy kiss, and he said he'd be happy to make it a reality.

Dressed in a fitted black dress just above my knees, sheer pantyhose, high-heeled black pumps, I felt sexy and charged. I met him in the building's elevator. He smiled at me and looked me up and down, undressing me with his eyes. When the doors shut and elevator climbed one floor, he hit the stop button.

"What are you doing?" I asked, both nervous and excited, knowing he was playing this game.

He stepped towards me, came in close, put his hand over my mouth and told me to be quiet.

"I am going to give you what you desire. I could tell when you came onto the elevator that you need a man. You are going to be my sexy slut."

He pulled me in close and grabbed my ass, caressing my body. He seemed different, just like a stranger.

"I'm not going to hurt you. This is just between you and me."

His hands moved to my breasts. I gasped.

"Mmm. You've got a fantastic body, you know that? I felt myself getting hard when you came onto the elevator. I am going to make you feel things as your body betrays you."

He slid his hands under my dress, pulling down my pantyhose, pushing aside my lace panties to enter a finger into my pussy.

"Wrap your left leg around my waist, " he ordered as he rhythmically moved his finger in and out, sliding his finger up and down my slit, stopping at my clit.

"You're getting wet..."

I tried to protest but nothing would come out. It had been a while since I'd felt a man's touch. My heart beat faster. I wrapped my leg around his waist as he unzipped his pants, pulled his boxers down, and let them both slide to his ankles. He pulled out a thick, hard cock and placed my hand on it.

"Stroke me," he ordered. I nervously placed my hand on his cock, moving it up and down while he moaned. He backed me against the elevator wall and placed his fingers in my mouth, ordering me to suck on his fingers. I liked this, this feeling of being taken. He opened a wrapper and slid a condom onto his hard cock.

"I'm going to fuck you. You're mine. Do you understand?"

I could feel a combination of fear and excitement wash through me while he entered me, pumping in and out, grunting as he pulled my hair. I grabbed his toned ass as he pushed into me, my leg wrapped around his waist. He pushed against me, pinning my arms against the wall. I let out a gasp. Adrenaline pulsed through my body as he held me in place. I wanted to run but at the same time, I wanted him to fill me, to release into me.

"Your pussy is nice and tight. It feels so good. Don't be scared. Just let it go," he whispered in my ear, sounding more like my boss and less of the stranger in the game.

I closed my eyes and took a few deep breaths, in and out. My body relaxed and I let go of my fear. I felt myself pulsate, my whole body in a wave of orgasm. He unpinned my arms, moving his hands down my body, stopping to caress my breasts and gave me a deep kiss. I felt his body tense as he exploded into me. He relaxed onto me for a moment. We collected ourselves, coming out of a collective haze.

"Pull up your panties and stockings," he demanded as he dressed.

He released the stop button on the elevator and pushed one for the top floor.

Our fantasy elevator tryst was the start of what would be a steamy relationship we had to keep secret from our colleagues.

~

"My First Menage a Trois"
By, Elizabeth Cane

Every Thursday night since I've known him, my husband has been playing hockey with a bunch of guys.

My husband is a cute enough guy and I really love him. Last year, a really cute guy in his late twenties moved from Toronto and joined the team.

He has the bluest eyes, dimples, and a fantastic ass!

I sort of developed a crush on Derrick and started to fantasize about him when my husband was out of town and I'd be left to get the job done with my trusty vibrator! I also started to hang around the hockey rink a bit more. One night, we went for drinks after the game. I made sure to wear my tightest jeans and my stiletto boots and a top that showed some cleavage. Derrick was definitely checking me out. And I flirted back.

My husband noticed and mentioned something on the way home. He seemed kind of jealous but at the same time, flattered that a younger teammate would think his wife was hot.

"So, honey, I've been noticing you've been coming to the games a lot more since Derrick came on the team...and you guys seem to hit it off.

Should I be worried?" he joked on the car ride home. I was a bit tipsy from a few glasses of wine at the bar.

"Umm...Well, Derrick is a good looking guy..."

My husband sighed as he turned into the driveway. I thought that was the end of the discussion. But, a few nights later, when we were lying in bed after a particularly hot session of sex, my husband asked me what I wanted for my birthday.

I didn't want a necklace or a spa treatment or new robe.

"Honey, I've been thinking about what you said about Derrick. I was thinking we could celebrate your birthday with him at Chez Martine. What do you think?"

I wasn't really sure where this was going but Chez Martine was the most posh and romantic spot in town. I agreed and the next day, went shopping for a sexy black dress that showed off my curves, some sky high stilettos and sexy lace lingerie, even if it's just to get Derrick into some innocent flirting.

When we got to the restaurant, Derrick looked me up and down. My husband was dealing with the valet so it was just the two of us.

"My, birthday girl, you look good enough to eat," said Derrick.

I blushed, not sure how to respond. It had been a while since a man other than my husband so overtly flirted with me. He pulled me in for a hug and moved his hands down to my shapely ass, kissing me on the lips. I swear I would have dragged him into the ladies room to ravage him but at that moment my husband arrived.

We decided to have some drinks before dinner and I sat at the bar between the two guys. Derrick slipped his hand on my stockinged knee and caressed my leg. I ordered champagne to calm my nerves.

My husband kissed me while Derrick continued to move his hand, ever so slightly up my thigh. I was so turned-on, and simultaneously nervous. I gulped my champagne and ordered another glass. After my third was finished, I felt tipsy so we moved to the table where my husband ordered an expensive cabernet.

Derrick was openly flirting with me by now and said, "Damn, you are one lucky bastard! Your wife is so sexy."

When my husband left to go to the bathroom, Derrick leaned over to kiss me, nibbling on my lips and slipping his tongue in my mouth. We were deeply kissing when my husband came back to the table...but to my surprise he didn't seem to mind. In fact, he took my hand and put it on his pants to show me he was hard. I was really excited to see a side of my husband I hadn't known; turned on because another man was all over me.

We polished off the bottle of wine. I barely had an appetite or any inhibitions at this point. Derrick continued to flirt with me over dinner, sliding his hand again up my leg, this time, stopping on my now, very wet panties. While my husband watched him, Derrick ran his fingers across my panties, slipping inside them to caress my mound, sliding his fingers into my wetness with his thumb on my clit.

My husband watched my mouth, as I tried to control my moans in a public place. I was breathless as he moved his fingers in and out. I grabbed onto the tablecloth and, staring into Derrick's eyes, and had a leg shaking orgasm. My husband leaned in and gave me a kiss on the lips.

A moment later, a waiter came by, I tried to act as if nothing happened, but I'm sure we looked out of sorts from the waiter's expression. They calmly ordered filet mignons and I a salmon dish, which when it arrived, I could barely touch.

I excused myself to go to the restroom. Derrick followed me. When we got to the hallway near the restrooms, he grabbed me close to him, moving his hands over my full breasts.

I sighed and we started to kiss deeply. We came back to the table, flushed. When the waiter asked for our dessert order, my husband winked and said smiling, "I think we will be having that at our place. Does that sound good to you, Derrick?"

We were all too drunk to drive anywhere, and being responsible horny adults, we called an Uber cab. We piled into the backseat, laughing. I was in the middle between Derrick and my husband. They both put a hand on my knee. My husband started to kiss me deeply as Derrick moved his hand to cup my breast. My husband played with my other breast. The Uber driver watched in the rearview mirror.

Derrick moved his hand inside my bra to pinch my hard nipple. I turned to face him and he kissed me deeply. I realized then, perhaps a little slow to do so, that my husband's birthday present to me would be my first threesome.

When we arrived at our house, my husband paid the driver as Derrick and I stood by the front door, making out like two teens on a date. He moved my hand down to see how hard he was and I was delighted to feel his size. Just thinking that I would have a new cock in me, and my husband watching was sensational.

I fumbled with the lock and we stumbled inside. My husband followed us, stopping at our bar to open a bottle of champagne. More alcohol; I wasn't certain if I needed anymore and I hoped they would stay sober enough to last awhile, but my I knew husband held his liquor well.

Derrick unzipped my dress, which fell to the floor. I was standing in my sexy lace bra, panties, and stockings. I let my long dark hair tumble down my shoulders. Derrick pulled me towards the couch and I straddled him. He reached to unhook my bra and brought his lips to my hard nipples. Twirling one tongue around my left nipple, he rolled the other nipple in his long fingers. My husband sat down on the couch sipping champagne and caressed my hair. I was in heaven.

I unzipped Derrick's jeans and he slipped out of them, his black boxer briefs tented by his nine inches of hardness. I grabbed his delicious ass and pulled his briefs down, pulling his cock into my mouth. While I sucked and licked Derrick's thick hardness, my husband had his own pants off, stroking his cock as he watched me pleasure his friend. I reached over to help my husband stroke his cock while I tasted Derrick's.

After a few minutes, we traded places. I had my husband in my mouth and was stroking Derrick. I was so wild with lust. I wanted both men in my mouth so I pulled them towards me. I sucked and licked both of them, their balls and up both their shafts. We were ecstatic. My husband came, exploding all over my breasts. Derrick whispered he wanted to be inside me. My husband nodded. I took Derrick's hand and led him upstairs to the master bedroom.

While my husband stood in the doorway and watched, Derrick slipped on a condom and made love to me, teasing me with his cock, kissing me deeply and bringing me to crashing waves of orgasms.

My husband was hard again and stroking his cock. I motioned for him to join us. Derrick turned me over and brushed his hands over my ass as my husband caressed my throbbing, drenched pussy. Derrick teased my tight ass with his hard cock. As my husband slid into my pussy, Derrick slid into my ass. We moved together until we all came. I have never felt so filled. I feel asleep in Derrick's arms with my husband's head on my chest.

This was the best birthday gift a girl could ever have.

"Stripper Fantasy"

By Elizabeth Cane

I'm one of those girls who married my college boyfriend pretty soon after graduation. We met on our first day registering for classes, so I haven't exactly had much sexual experience.

As my thirty-fifth birthday approached, I began to fantasize about stripping in front of a room full of hot businessmen. How did I go from soccer mom to a woman who got turned on by the idea of entertaining a room full of guys?

When I look back, it started when my divorced friend Melanie invited me to try a pole dancing class with her. A lot of women were doing it for exercise so I figured I'd give it a try. For the first class, I wore some yoga pants and a fairly loose tank top. I wasn't feeling especially sexy after giving birth to three kids; now eleven, nine, and four years old. But, as I started to move my body during the warm up, I could almost feel my sensuality blossom. I grazed my hands over my voluptuous breasts, feeling my curves, through my wavy dark hair. By the time we got to try "Firefly," our first pole trick, I was in my element. The pulsating music just brought out a new side in me.

I signed up for six sessions and the next day, bought myself some very short booty shorts and a tank top that left nothing to the imagination. I also ordered some six-inch stripper shoes; I was going to do this all the way.

Within a few classes, I noticed a difference even when I wasn't at the studio. I traded in my "mom" jeans for a pair of skintight skinnies and my sneakers for some sexy high-heeled boots.

I started to wear my hair down instead of pulled back and wore makeup. My husband didn't really notice the change but the guys in the local coffee shop sure did! I loved the attention. One night, the girls in the studio and I decided to take a field trip to a strip club in a nearby town.

The strippers climbed and shimmied down their poles in nothing less than an athletic performance. Their moves mesmerized me. Right then and there, I knew I had to try my hand on the stage. Before we left, I met the manager who told me I could come for an audition the next afternoon.

I hired a babysitter and took off for the club in my shortest, tightest booty shorts that just hugged my toned but curvy ass. I sported an extra small tank top that showed off the DD cups my husband had bought me after our third child was born!

The lights were dimmed as I approached the stage. The manager put on some rhythmic music with a strong bass. I sauntered to the pole, teasing him with my sexy moves. I ran my hands over my firm breasts, my small waist, lightly brushing over the front of my shorts and my toned body. I wanted to give that manager a raging hard-on! I ran my tongue across my full lips, tasting the cherry lip-gloss I had just applied. I shimmied up the pole, all the way to the top, wrapping my legs around it.

I let go of one leg at a time and did amazing pole tricks, the kind that make men fantasize what it would be like to have you in their bed. I knew the manager was more than impressed and the sexy, hunky bartender whistled.

After my fifteen-minute performance, I had an impulse to strip. I strutted across the stage in my six-inch heels, stopping to crouch near the manager.

"I have another treat for you," I whispered.

Both the manager and the bartender could not take their eyes off me. To the beat of the pulsating music, I slowly took off my tank top to reveal spectacular tits in a lacy bra. I danced and ran my hands down my body before slipping off my panties to reveal my fully waxed pussy. I knew bottomless wasn't going to fly in a club that served alcohol but I was fulfilling my fantasy.

I let my bra straps slip down my shoulders before removing my bra to reveal my full breasts and hard nipples.

" You are so fucking hot!" said the manager. "I'm going to bill you as our new "MILF" stripper. Guys will line up to see you!"

The manager handed me a g-string and some pasties. "Wear these tomorrow and be here by seven. You are going to be a star!"

After feeding the kids the next night, I told my husband I was going to my book club and headed for the club where I met the other girls.

Most of the strippers were in their early twenties. They welcomed me like an older sister. One of the youngest girls said, "Damn, girl, you've got a great body. You need a stripper name!" We decided on Samantha since I had always thought that was a sophisticated name.

I slipped on a short skirt and blouse with the pasties and g-string underneath. I watched the other girls work the pole from backstage, their nubile young bodies driving the men crazy.

The manager told me I was going to be the main act so I'd be going on at nine o'clock. He announced, "Introducing our newest dancer, Samantha, soccer mom by day, sex goddess by night!"

When I looked into the audience, right in the front row was my husband's boss, Mr. Wilkinson, a very good-looking grey-haired gentleman. I always thought he was really sexy.

I was a bit unnerved that he might tell my husband, but when he winked at me, I knew all was good. I stared at him the whole time I danced. He stared at me with lust in his eyes. I worked the pole better than I had ever done. I felt the eyes of all the guys on me. After my pole routine, I moved towards the front of the stage and gave my husband's boss quite a performance.

His client commented as the two sipped beers, "Shit, I think you need to give my friend a lap dance," and he slipped a hundred dollar bill into my bra beneath my slightly unbuttoned blouse.

Tracey, the next dancer, was being introduced on the stage while the other guys applauded me. I hopped down the stage and placed a finger on Mr. Wilkinson's lip and grabbed his hand.

"What about that lap dance? *But it's gotta stay between us,*" I whispered.

"Mind if I watch?" asked the client, a good-looking guy around forty, as he played with his wedding ring.

"Come with me."

I motioned and brought the men to a private back room. The idea that my husband's multi-millionaire boss was turned on by me was driving me wild. I felt my pussy throbbing.

One of the girls had shown me how to flip on the music. As the beat started, I led Mr. Wilkinson to a chair. His client stood near the doorway. I told him to sit with his legs closed and stared straight into his eyes, walking around him and dragging my fingers through his thick hair.

I lightly brushed his chest while I explained the rules. He couldn't touch me.

I switched between looking at him and looking down at my own body, touching myself. I imagined his hands all over me as I touched myself, rolling my head and running my fingers through my wavy hair. I moved towards him, my crotch almost touching his knee, leaning in as if I were going to kiss him but then pulling away. I moved back and circled my hips slowly, closing my eyes and then walking cat-like towards him. Now was time for my first lap dance.

I swayed between Wilkinson's legs, bumping and grinding against his hardness. I turned my body away from him, between his legs before bending down to sit on his lap, grinding my bottom slowly against his hard cock.

I moved away from him to pose so he could take a long look at my body before I slipped off my skirt, revealing my g-string. I moved in closer, practically sitting in his lap, sensually leaning in to breathe a hot breath over his ear. I was so beyond turned on and let out a moan.

I softly brushed my lips against his neck before moving away to dance for him, moving my hands over my body before unbuttoning my blouse. I caressed my full breasts over the pasties.
The client was also turned on.

"Shit, man. So freaking hot."
Staring straight into Mr. Wilkinson's big dark eyes, I continued to caress myself, crawling and then mounting him again, this time facing him, to grind my pussy against him before leaning over to give him a kiss on the cheek.

I whispered in his ear, asking if he enjoyed our performance before moving my hand to brush against his hard cock. I know I wasn't supposed to let this go further but I was so turned on and by the looks of things, so was he! I gently pumped his cock through his expensive dress pants, a nice eight or so inches I felt.

It had been so long since I touched or even looked at another guy's cock and I was hungry! I unbuckled and unzipped his pants to reveal the thick, hard cock, the tip peeking through his briefs.

It had been equally as long since I had another man's dick in my mouth. I slid off his lap onto my knees and licked the tip while he gasped. Sliding his pants and briefs to his knees, I moved my tongue up and down the shaft, circling the tip and sucking on his beautiful eight and a half inches. I gently licked and played with his manscaped balls before sliding my tongue back up the shaft, staring into his eyes the whole time.

By now, the client had his own dick out of his pants and was stroking his hardness. I devoured all of Wilkinson's cock, feeling it pump into the back of my throat, touching my tonsils, tasting his pre-cum while he stroked my hair.

"Damn, David is one lucky fuck!"

I looked up naughtily, sucking, almost gagging before I felt him release into me. I swallowed every drop of his salty sweet cum.

"Oh, David never gets this special treatment, Mr. Wilkinson!" I exclaimed.

"You can call me Blake," he said as I moved back into his lap to give him a deep kiss.

"So, 'Samantha,' I have a proposition for you." he took a pause, staring into my eyes, thinking abut asking something that I could tell was a bit dangerous. "What if you become my private dancer?"

I didn't answer right away, but let the implications of what he asked settle in. After a moment, I was excited to think of the possibilities.

That night was the end of my job dancing in the club, but the start of my relationship with Mr. Wilkinson... *Blake*, which has now continued for many years.

Author: Skyler Knightley
Skyler Knightley is a complete nerd goddess by day and a rocker chick by night. You can find her hanging out backstage with alternative and indie rockers, collecting tales for her steamy stories. She melts over a man with smarts and a mysterious exterior. Her stories reflect her deepest, darkest secrets and desires. It's up to you to decide what's truth and what's fantasy.

"Boundaries"
By Skyler Knightley

I opened the box and stared down at all my friends and ran my fingers across a row of silk in all colors and the next row was of leathers. I licked my lips longingly then blew an enticing kiss toward the perfect specimen already shackled behind me.

He couldn't see my note of affection, but I knew he heard the pucker of my lips and the sweet exhale of my breath. He quivered and shook against the cold, brick wall, my assistant had bound him to. He sucked his pouty, bottom lip in between his top and bottom row of teeth then chewed nervously.

I waltzed toward him aggressively, staring for a moment at the beauty that stood before me.

I was glad I had chosen blue silk to cover his stormy eyes instead of my stereotypical red. I ran my finger toward his mouth and plucked his swollen lip from his teeth. My index finger lingered on that perfection of bee sting. I dwelled so long that he sucked in and drew my finger into his hot, wet mouth. Feeling his long tongue twist around my finger, caressing it like a child relishes a red lollipop.

I pulled it from his mouth with a mighty *"pop."*

I strolled my wet finger down his chin, along his beautiful, sculptured chest, stopping at his amazingly, and enticing belly button.

My assistant said he had been reluctant to strip down so quickly without seeing me first, but I never doubted my very persuasive subordinate. There's a reason why he had been with me for five years.

I bent down and blew cool air from my lovely's abdomen all the way up to his left pulse point on his neck. He reared his neck back like he was willingly waiting for me to bite him. He was already glistening with sweat from anticipation. I glanced down and his hard cock stood erect and wanting. I leaned forward, allowing the silk of my white blouse to brush his chest hair. I breathed for a moment into his ear, watching as the sweat turned to chills.

"Is this what you thought it would be?"

I whispered into his ear. He licked his lips and swallowed before he spoke, "Not exactly but I'm not complaining."

I slowly moved to the other ear, "What were you expecting?" He swallowed again and arched his back, "I don't know but I was hoping to see you first I guess."

I grabbed his earlobe with my teeth and slightly pulled. My lips danced back toward his ear opening, "Oh you will, but I need to explore you first."

I ran my finger along his beautiful jaw line. He was pure perfection. There was no doubt about that. I loved the way stubble danced across his statue chiseled jawbones. To have this much beauty waltz into my clutches on a silver platter was almost too much.

I had been doing this sort of entertainment for some time but no one had ever captivated me like this one.

I was perfectly content just staring at him. Touching him was a whole other level of euphoria. When I walked into the room, he was the last person I expected to see. If you haven't figured it out yet, I *knew him*. He was the man who haunted every aspect of my being for the past two years.

He didn't know I did this. The person he thought he knew me as was a lie and maybe that was part of the problem. He thought me to be the quiet librarian type. I kept up the persona, feeling that his bookish ways would be enthralled by my own grasp of classic literature. Our conversations were in depth and we often flirted, but nothing dramatic ever came to fruition except in my dreams. I wondered if I had exposed to him the true me would he have stuck around. I was too scared to ever do it, feeling that he would flee, rather than run into my open arms.

Needless to say, time and space made us drift apart, but there wasn't a day that didn't go by that I didn't fantasize about him. Now, before me, there he was...naked and ready for me to play with.

The irony that he stepped into my secret world was beyond anything I could comprehend. I had been given a gift and it wasn't anything that I dreamed of returning.

The brown leather straps around his wrists pulled tighter as I moved away from him.
I looked down and focused on the beauty of his absolutely magnificent dick pointed up at me.

I had always wondered what it looked like and my eyes soaked in every inch never wanting to forget a single, throbbing vein. He was luscious and astonishing, far beyond my imagination.

His head twisted back and forth, wandering what I was doing. I ran my hand through his soft hair to comfort him. My other hand rapidly grabbed his cock and held it tight. I bent down before him and sucked him into my mouth. He was silky smooth and I pulled the full length of him down my longing throat. He gasped at first then moaned in absolute nirvana. I smiled in the knowledge that I was the one making him continuously lament.

I licked him with the tip of my tongue, starting at his wide shaft and slowly conquering his perfect pink tip. I immediately swallowed him back down and his quivering response sent me into my own ecstasy. His reactions were so enticing that I finally decided to reveal everything to him.

I pulled my black leather pencil skirt up to my waist, wrapped my legs tightly around him, and then leisurely melted onto his quivering cock. His longing moan broke into a masculine groan as my muscles wrapped around every massive inch of him.

I released his hands from their bonds so he could hold me up. His hips instantly bucked forward, trying to drive into me deeper. I gasped, digging my red high-heeled shoes into his lower back, as his movements became more rapid. I ran my fingers through his beautiful, soft brown hair.

I buried my face in his neck, finding his pulse point, then bit down lightly. The smell of his sweat soaked body sent me into a rage of desire. He was intoxicating like a perfect ocean that was ebbing and flowing all around you. I reluctantly pulled back from his neck and stared where his eyes were still encased in blue silk. I wanted him to come, knowing it was me that had made him feel such intense pleasure.

I gently slid the silk upward and our eyes immediately locked. We simultaneously came as soon as we saw each other. A smile crossed our flushed faces as we shook furiously in each other's arms from bliss. I placed both hands on the sides of his face and kissed him longingly. He returned the kiss without hesitation as his cock quivered inside of me.

"I finally found you." He said, fighting for breath.

I smiled at him skeptically, "What does that mean?"

"When I heard a rumor that you might be here, I had to find out and here you are exactly where I have wanted you to be for months." The look in his eyes was filled with absolute love.

"But how?" I was too shocked to say much else.

"That's a story for another day. When can I see you again?" He placed a lock of my hair behind my ear.

"Whenever you want. You can come here whenever you want." My words were stuttered at the thought that he wanted to see me again.

"No, not here. I'm not going to make your stop your...business but I do think we should draw up some boundaries. You game?" His grey eyes twinkled with excitement.

"No games with you. This was the last one." I touched my forehead to his.

A pout crossed his lips, "No. The game we started tonight needs to continue, that's a boundary."

"Deal." We kissed to seal the deal and I couldn't wait to get him home to show him all the other toys hiding in my bedroom. There would definitely be a plethora of boundaries there.

~

"Three Is Trouble"
By, Skyler Knightley

I put down my beaten acoustic guitar on the nearby stand and raked my hands through my wavy brown hair. The run down club, *The Nightmare*, was packed tonight. The audience seemed to be mainly female. A smirk crossed my lips when I thought that maybe they had come to just see me play; a good looking guitar playing young guy. I crossed over to the bar where a Jameson on the rocks patiently waited for me. I noticed a nice looking couple at the end of the bar staring at me.

I had seen them here for the past few weeks and they seemed to be glued to me every time I played a set. The man was a corporate type, probably in his late thirties. His style was immaculate and very "metro" compared to my laid back Hipster style.

The lady beside him seemed a bit younger and a lot less business like. She reminded me of Scarlett Johansson with perfect pouty lips and engaging eyes. I returned to my drink suddenly realizing that I, myself, was staring. Attractive couples didn't come into places like this. I wondered what they were looking for and what had brought them here.

Just as I was about to jump off the bar stool, someone plucked me by the sleeve of my thrift store denim shirt. I turned to see "Mr. Business Man" smiling at me. He looked nervous but the creases in his forehead showed determination.

"Excuse me. I'm sorry to bother you but I was wondering if I could talk to you for a moment." His blue eyes sparkled almost with mischief.

"Sure. How can I help you?" My interest was piqued and I wasn't quite sure what this guy could possibly want with a twenty-something bar musician.

He studied the ground for a moment then

jumped off the proverbial cliff he had been desperately avoiding.

"See that gorgeous woman over there. That's my wife. We stumbled into here one night because she heard your voice as we were passing by. She's got a *thing* for musicians. Since then, she hasn't missed any of your sets. It's safe to say that she's got a tremendous crush on you. She thinks you're like a cross between a young Hugh Grant and that guy that plays Superman."

A smile spread across my lips filled with shyness and cockiness all at the same time, "That's good to know but I'm not quite sure where you're heading with this."

Mr. Business Man kicked the nearby leg of the bar stool then spit it out, "She wants to have sex with you."

If I had been drinking, I would have spit all over the anxious man, "Excuse me?"

This time he laughed, "Don't freak out. She's beautiful, right? I know you think she's hot because I just saw you checking her out. It would just be with her. I will be nowhere around. Trust me, three is trouble. This is her freebie card and she wants to use it on you. So, uh, what do you think?"

I signaled the bartender for another drink. I didn't know what to say. I looked over at where she was sitting.

"Listen man, this is something she's wanted to do for a long time. We've been looking for the right guy for months then we run into you, Mr. Perfect, in her eyes. It isn't going to be complicated. No names, no addresses, no phone numbers. Once it happens, you will never hear from us again. Just all fun. Trust me." As my confidence waned, his began to wax.

I gulped my drink down locking eyes with the hot blonde. She licked her lips slowly and leaned seductively onto the bar, "I'm in. There's a green room slash dressing room in the back. Does that work?" Mr. Business Man smiled knowing he had obtained his goal.

"Backstage after a performance. It's exactly what she wants. Wait here."

He sauntered away from me to whisper in her ear. A soft, sexy smile fell across those succulent lips. I shifted slightly, feeling myself getting hard from the absolute smoldering glances she kept throwing my way. I wasn't sure what I was doing but I sure the hell knew I wanted to do it.

They both walked over to me and she immediately leaned in, kissed my cheek, and whispered into my ear, "You're going to be everything I want and I'm going to rock your world."

Her hand caressed my inner thigh then worked its way up to grasp my hardness through my black Levis. Her eyebrows shot up and she was obviously impressed by how hard and how big I was. I took her hand and led her into the back, leaving her corporate husband to drink away at the bar.

The back dressing room was actually better than the bar itself. There was a big couch and dozens of mirrors. As soon as the door closed, she crashed into my lips. I pulled into my arms so she could wrap her legs around me.

I am 6'4" and she was at least a foot shorter than me. Her kisses were deep and her tongue hinted at what she wanted to do to me and what she wanted me to do to her. I sat down on the sofa with a perfect view of us reflected in the mirror.

Her lips danced down my neck, finding the pulse point and biting down hard. I threw my head back, not in pain but in absolute ecstasy. No one had done that to me before and I didn't want it to be the last time. As she worshipped my neck, her fingers worked on loosening my belt and unzipping my jeans. My fingers brushed against my hard on still encased in my briefs. I bit my bottom lip. It had been far too long since a woman had touched me, let alone a woman this hot.

She shimmied down my long legs so that she was on her knees in front of me. The corner of her mouth cocked in anticipation of what she was about to do. She gently released me from my briefs and immediately put me into her mouth. The sensation running through my body danced down my spine as she sucked me deeply up and down then twirled her tongue around the tip before beginning again. Her big eyes didn't look away, enjoying every moment that I responded to her intimate caresses. She plucked me from her mouth with a pop then licked up and down.

I was breathless and ready to go further. I hopped up and moved her toward the mirrored dressing table. I turned her around so she was facing the mirror. She immediately grasped the edge of the table and thrust her ass back into me. I pulled the bottom of her dress up to her waist and smiled to see no panties present. This was going to be perfect for both us. I could completely see her and she could completely see me.

We wanted to watch and that was exactly what we both were going to get. I licked my index finger and ran it up her beautifully wet pussy.

I plucked the finger back into my mouth; so curious about what she tasted like. The flavor of her enticed me so I instantaneously bent down to savor her more with my tongue. She tasted like coconut with the hint of the clean ocean air. Her legs began to shake as my tongue twirled and teased near the hard bead that demanded my attention. Her knuckles grew white as she clutched the hard surface, wanting to drive her nails completely through. Her wetness was running down her soft thighs showing how ready she was for me to make her cum.

I drew the sensitive, trembling bud into my mouth, sucking slowly, and then biting down viciously. She screamed out, enraptured by the mix of pleasure and pain. I nursed the wound with my tongue causing expletives of bliss to fall from her perfect lips. I toyed with her, loving the way she smelled and tasted. I grasped my hard on, needing to reach the level that I had driven her to. With one more, sweet succulent suck, she came hard, gasping with her legs barely able to hold her in place.

I stood up then stood her up. I gently stripped her dress away, kissing her neck and returning the pulse point bite that she had given me earlier. The sound that escaped was a cross between a laugh and a cry. She looked into the mirror and studied me as one hand found its way to her beautiful hard nipple and the other massaged between her legs, keeping her damp and ready to go. I could tell she wanted to say something but couldn't. All words had escaped her. I bent her back over and she obliged by spreading her legs wider than before. I was extremely hard and absolutely ready to make her come again.

I flirted my cock along her wet opening, teasing the tip near the entry but not going in. She cried out in frustration, her lip caught between her teeth, feeling nothing but absolute need to be satisfied again.

I grinned wickedly as our eyes locked and slammed into her. The rhythm we both demanded was hard and we never looked away from each other. Her hips pressed back into me just as quickly as I pushed forward into her. My hands moved forward to find her remarkable breasts.

They were so round and full. I tormented her nipples, refusing to let them be anything but hard.

They grew red but I could tell by the unbridled breaths coming from her mouth, she wanted nothing more than the pain I was giving her. Her muscles wrapped around my cock tightly, refusing to let go.

My own breath became short and I loved every moment she responded to me. I pushed harder and her body just starting replying without her even knowing what she was doing. I thrusted deeply one last time and she cried out as the second orgasm rocked her body into uncontrollable shivers. I crashed into her, emptying utterly inside her with complete abandon.

I helped her stand up, pulling her into me, tenderly kissing her neck and softly massaging her amazing curves. I loved how the aftershocks vibrated her and made her absolutely compliant to my every caress. I massaged her breasts soothingly and petted the sensitivity between her legs. She inhaled and I could feel her rising again. She withdrew my hand from between her legs then turned to me.

"Listen handsome, you just gave me two of the most amazing orgasms I've ever had but you better not give me a third or I just might leave my husband for you. Two is no strings, three is trouble."

Her eyes sparkled from the afterglow. When she left, I never heard from her or her husband again, as promised. However, in the weeks that followed, more and more corporate looking men started bringing their wives to the bar.

You won't hear me complaining.

~

Author: Jessica Lucas
Jessica Lucas is a woman who knows what she wants in life, and in a romantic partner. A true vixen in bed, a force at work, and a woman who delights in experiencing the unexpected in her writing, and in her own life. Many of her stories come from personal experiences, and she is always open to divulging the secrets that are behind the door to her bedroom.

"The Hammock"
By, Jessica Lucas

A gorgeous orange sunset was on the horizon as I lounged in my balcony hammock. My Husband and I had taken a much-needed break from fast city life. Twelve-hour days, buzzing phones, and endless emails tossed aside, for beachside fruity drinks with umbrellas all day, and romantic candle lit dinners at night.

The weather was perfect; sun shining brightly on the beautiful tranquil waters creating shadows of light that appeared to dance with each ripple of the Caribbean water. A soft breeze ruffled my hair, as I laid completely relaxed watching the sunset on yet another perfect day.

The door slid open as my husband joined me on the patio. He did not move towards the empty hammock next to mine, instead he approached me. Taking one of my feet in his hands he began to massage them gently. The tension of work and life was slowly retreating from my body.

His hands moved with such precision, determined to send me into a sweet relaxed slumber. But sleep was not to be had this afternoon. His hands continued to massage my feet moving up to my calves and kneading them as well. My eyes were unable to stay open, and I placed my arms above my head, stretching them out to the hammock's edges.

A slight moan escaped my lips and that was his cue to continue. He did, but in an entirely different direction. Lifting my legs up on the hammock he slid his body opposite mine. My legs placed across his, spread open in front of him. My bathing suit bottoms were removed with ease and the massage continued; my thighs, calves, and feet became his playground.

A sudden jolt took me by surprise. My eyes flew open and I gasped. An ice cube had found its way into his hands and he was dragging it up and down the inside of my thighs. The cold felt delicious against my hot sun touched skin.

"Cold, darling?" he asked. I giggled in response, unable to stop or hide how much I enjoyed the sublime torture.

"Keep going," I whispered. He continued. The first ice cube was melting and another quickly replacing it. No longer satisfied with my legs, he plucked my bathing suit top from me, throwing it on the ground of the balcony. It lay there, absent from my breasts that were now being exposed to the cold chill of the ice cube. My nipples instantly grew hard as he swirled the ice cube in circles around them.

He had to straddle the hammock to reach my breasts properly with his hands, his feet planted firmly on the ground. His mouth found it's way too.

The cold from the ice cube was being replaced with his hot mouth against my nipples. The change in temperature caused sensations to run through my body. A deep want for additional teasing, more pleasure to be found in his atypical lovemaking ideas.

As his mouth continued to suckle and tease my increasingly hard nipples his hands found their way beneath my legs.

A circular motion was applied to my clit, the water from the melted ice cube still lingering his fingers mingled with my own hot juices. Wetter I grew as his fingers continued to massage the very spot that sends me into a storm of pleasure.

I grew eager for his cock and managed to move one of my legs so I could reach his cock with my toes. I took my toes and rubbed up against his growing bulge.

Tiny bits of pressure I applied, and with each I could feel him twitch beneath me. "I want your mouth on me," he whispered into my ear as he took his mouth away from my breasts. I pushed him back on the hammock, and removed his trunks. His cock stood hard in front of me and I smiled knowing just how excited he was from giving me pleasure.

I took his cock in my hand, caressing it up and down for a moment; first slowly and then with greater force. His head tilted back and I bent over at the waist and placed the tip of my tongue against his knob. Tiny flicks I made, small circles, and then opened my mouth wide and swallowed the whole of his tonsil tickler. His entire cock inside of my mouth I swallowed, the back of my throat flexing against him.

The sound he made was unintelligible, like a wild animal in the throes of ecstasy. I did it again, and again, at the same time swirling my tongue around his shaft.

Moving on, I glided my mouth up and down his fully engorged penis. But that was not enough.

I considered grabbing an ice cube, and then decided my warm tongue would be more enjoyable. He was so hard I knew he could explode at any moment, and the amount of pleasure I wanted to give him was not complete. I made my way between his legs, just below his balls, and licked. Licked the one part of Him that I knew would drive him into frenzy. Would cause his body to convulse and make him have to hold out from coming straight into the air. And it worked.

The minute my tongue touched the special spot beneath his balls, trailing along it slowly. Pulling away only to place quick snaps of my tongue there again to receive the same response.

He was ready to be inside of me, and I wanted to feel his hardness, feel it touch the very insides of me reach the back and poke at me, dying to go further inside.

I lounged back on the hammock, ready for him to climb on top of me any which way he may manage. But he did something else. Pulling me towards him by my waist he put one of my legs beneath his and alternated with his own. We looked like a pair of scissors coming together and that was just what we planned to do.

His cock glided in side of me, the warmth and wetness of my pussy was engulfing every inch of him. The hammock swayed as he began to move in and out of me. The intensity grew as the hammock swayed more and more; the sound of the wood creaking from the force rang out in the air. I bent my leg in order to grip him tighter and he responded with deep thrusts. He was able to reach depths of me I did know existed in this position. Every inch of him lost inside of me and I grew wetter with every second.

The sun made its final descent over the horizon just as my body found its release. I felt spasms' with him inside of me, crying out with my pleasure. He was not finished yet.

His hard cock continued to glide in and out of me, the ripples of pleasure continuing to move through my body at the same time. He reached his hand beneath my legs and the moment he touched me, swollen and hot, I came again.

The hammock swaying made me even dizzier with pleasure, and the feel of the woven fabric on my body gave way to sensations running all over my skin while they continued to run through my body.

I was in ecstasy, and the gorgeous man across from me had made it possible. Now it was his turn, and I wanted to taste him. I pulled away from him, his penis releasing itself from the grip of my tight pussy.

I maneuvered myself up on all fours, carefully keeping my balance in the endlessly swinging hammock. I placed his cock back in my mouth, felt it harden even more as my tongue made waves around it as my mouth moved up and down with a ferocious vigor.

"I'm going to cum," he said through clenched teeth.

I smiled but did not stop. I used my hand to grip his cock hard and moved it along the bottom of his shaft as my mouth and tongue continued to tease and pleasure the top.

I felt the inevitable twitch of his cock, and without further warning he poured into my mouth. The saltiness covering my throat as I swallowed it in one gulp satisfied at the pleasure I had given him and he in return to me.

The hammock's sway came to a stop, as we were lying wrapped in one another's arms, the night sky beckoning and the first stars were appearing in the sky.

~

"On Your Knees" (Part one)
By Jessica Lucas

I am very good at following directions; so when I received a note at work today stating I should be at the Palms Hotel at 7:00 p.m. wearing a short black skirt, white blouse, and no panties I obliged accordingly.

I checked-in at the front desk and the key was waiting for me. I was told to use the name *Trixie Giveth*, much to the amusement of the hotel staff. They were so kind as to let me know breakfast was served from 7:00 a.m. to 11 a.m. in the hotel restaurant, as if they actually believed I would still be there in the morning.

The room was located on the top floor, and I rode the elevator with great anticipation. The elevator was made of glass, and the view of the atrium could be seen as I climbed higher and higher up. When the bell rang signaling I had arrived at my floor I nearly jumped from the startling interruption of quiet I had been experiencing. Lost in my own thoughts over what I would find when I arrived at room 1218.

Adjusting my skirt, smoothing out my blouse, and applying my red lipstick one last time, and with a quick lick of my lips I knocked on the door. He opened it wearing absolutely nothing. His penis already partially erect and the room shrouded in a calm light of grey and blue thanks to the sheer window panels letting in the last of the Summer sun.

He said nothing as I stood there, a smile on my face while my hands gripped my handbag tighter with slight nervousness. A tilt of his head motioned me towards the bed. I walked slowly, examining the room.

There were candles lit on the tables and over and around the marble fireplace located on the center wall of the room. A fire was lit, making the room unusually warm. It made me want to remove my clothes and lay next to it, his body pressed to mine, smelling of sweet sweat.

I made my way to the side of the bed and stood there as he watched my every move. He kissed me hard on the mouth, his tongue swirling inside it. His stubble scratched my face, sending shivers of pain and pleasure through me. His kiss lasted for minutes, devouring every crevice of my mouth, nipping with his teeth on my lips. When he pulled away I was breathless, and wanting more.

His mouth moved to the nape of my neck, kissing and licking me along the edge of my collarbone and up to my ear. Tiny flicks against my earlobe caused a moan to escape my lips, and when he sucked on them I about melted to the ground.

His hands reached for my blouse buttons and undid each one slowly and with precision. My shirt dropped to the ground behind me, revealing my luscious breasts to him. He took full advantage of the fact that I had not worn a bra this evening.

My nipples grew hard at his touch, even as his mouth was warm against them. He did not suck on me. Instead, he *bit* me. Tiny, soft bites on my nipples as his hands grabbed my ass and gripped me hard. Having teased my nipples and following a massage of my breasts, he stood back. His cock was rock hard in front of me. Every beautiful inch of it on display for me to see and admire. What could only have been seconds felt like minutes, as he remained silent, staring at me in my half-dressed state.

The silence far too much for me to handle any longer I spoke to him.

"I am waiting for directions," I said.

"You are a very good girl, aren't you?" he responded. "Always following directions as you should." I nodded. A smile escaping even as I tried to act very serious. He grabbed a pillow from the bed and threw it at my feet between the two of us.

"On your knees," he demanded of me.

I happily obliged; his cock now directly in front of my face. I flicked my tongue against the tip, feeling naughty for doing something he had not directed me to.

"Put your mouth on my cock," he said. Opening my mouth wide I moved towards his hardness.

"No, just on the tip," he said when he noticed I was going in deep. I placed my lips around the tip of his cock, suckling it gently. My tongue was finding its way in circles.

"Now all of it," he spoke. I swallowed his cock whole. My mouth opening wide against his shaft and I took it all in my mouth. I could barely breathe, as I started moving up and down his shaft.

He was so hard that my mouth glided perfectly against him. With my lips moist and my tongue dancing along him with each stroke. I took my hand and placed it on the bottom of his shaft, and was swiftly chastised.

"No hands," he demanded. He grabbed my hand from his cock and held it tightly, eventually placing it behind him so I could grab his ass my second hand quickly joining.

I knelt there, my hands grabbing his behind as my mouth continued to devour every glorious Inch of his hard cock. I could feel myself growing wet between my legs. The excitement over his game mingling with the intense emotions I felt providing him pleasure. His head tilted back in pleasure as I continued to suck his cock, harder and faster with each up and down movement. He stepped back quickly, his cock removing itself from mouth.

He grabbed it with his hand and placed it between my breasts. Rubbing it between them he moaned with pleasure, his head titling back.

I looked down at my breasts, his cock between them, the head edging its way up towards my mouth. I put my chin in my chest as far as I could and licked the tip of his cock with my tongue.

Each time he moved it through my breasts up towards my mouth it was met with my tongue and a deep growl escaped his lips.

"Stand up," he said. I stood, and he pulled my skirt down around my ankles. I instinctively stepped out of it, kicking my heels to the side.

"Kiss me, hard," he whispered as he grabbed my ass with his hands. I kissed him deeply, my tongue performing the same technique it had on his cock inside his mouth and on his lips. He lifted one of my legs and draped it across his hip. His cock found its way to my wet pussy.

"Use me to pleasure yourself," he said.

I took his cock in my hand and rubbed it against my wetness. I applied pressure with it against my clit, and nearly screamed with pleasure. He slid across me with ease, eliciting pleasure in me while he found it as well in the feel of me against him. He put my leg down and turned me around to bend over the bed. His hard cock glided inside me, as he grabbed my hair and pulled. I screamed out, and placed my fingers between my legs to pleasure myself as he moved in and out of me. The double sensation flowed through my body.

"Your pussy is so tight and wet. I love fucking you," he whispered into my back as it arched to meet his thrusts more fully and deeply. "You give me so much pleasure."

"I love the feel of your hard cock inside of me," I responded. "Give me more, go deeper, harder, I want to feel every inch of you."

His thrusts became stronger, deeper, as his hands reached around my body and grabbed my breasts. He was using them for support as he moved further inside of me. I could feel the quivering of his cock as he held back the urge to cum.

I too was holding back, wanting us to find release together but not wanting the intense enjoyment to end quite yet.

"Flip over on your back so I can see you," he said.

I moved onto my back to let him inside of me but not until I grabbed his cock with my hands and feasted my mouth on it one last time. I could taste a small amount of him as it escaped the tip of his cock. I used my tongue to catch it as it moved down his shaft and licked my lips with it tasting the saltiness.

I pulled his head down and kissed him hard. The combination of him and me on my lips, and he sighed with delight. Pushing me back down onto the bed he picked me up at the hips and put his cock back inside of me. Everything went so quickly, as he moved in and out of me, breathing heavily and groaning as he felt me tighten against him.

Suddenly he pulled himself out and was straddled over me, his cock above my breasts and his hand moving along his penis while the other hand touched me. The instant he touched me, applied pressure to my clit, I came; over and over, uncontrollable spasms, shaking where I lay. Seconds later, his cock erupted on my tits, spilling all over them as he cried out.

He collapsed on the bed next to me, unable to speak just as I was.

~

"Bend Over As Far As You Can" (Part Two)
By Jessica Lucas

I woke up, half on top of him. The anticipation leading up to tonight, and the exertion it culminated in made us both need a quick catnap in order to prepare for what was coming next. Room Service arrived at the exact time he had planned for, and we indulged in pancakes covered in butter and pure maple syrup as the candle's continued to burn. The chocolate cake, with a side of raspberry chocolate sauce, beckoned me, but a knock on the door made me quickly forget the sweet taste it would have in mouth.

What was behind the door was even more enticing. Now, the story cannot continue without knowing exactly how it all came to be. A third person, waiting to be led into the room by the two of us deserves to have her story told, and telling it I fully plan on doing.

It all started about two weeks ago...

I am so nervous, nearly shaking, that I may topple down these stairs, as I do not think my feet can support my steps. One of my more adventurous friends recommended this bar, located in a basement of one of the fanciest movie palaces in the city, if not country. It is hard to believe that for years I have been coming to see films 100 feet or so above where I stand now and never knew what lurked below.

The stairwell is not lit well, but I can see ornate fixtures and the plush red carpet that lines the halls. One foot in front of the other and I am making my way down the stairs, I arrive at the coat check and a very young, and very seductive woman smiles at me.

"May I check your coat?" she says. My voice

cracking in an embarrassing fashion I answer her with a kind "yes" and hand it off.

"The bar is right through that door," she says, pointing to an enormous red curtain hanging from a door jam that is at least twenty-five feet tall to the left.

"Unless you are here for a movie. In that case, the theatre is upstairs," she adds.

Her assumption that I am in the wrong place is not far from the truth—and I appreciate her trying to save me from what horrors might lie beyond the red curtain. I am of course only kidding here, as I full well know what is in the bar and not only do I support it; I am hoping to join in this evening. That is, if I can get my voice to work long enough to try.

"I am in the right place. Thank you for your help," I say.

"No problem. Have fun," she says with a wicked smile.

I walk towards the ominous velvet curtain and push it aside to take a peek at where I will spend my evening. There are women everywhere, as there should be in a gay lounge.

But I am surprised at just how gorgeous each and every one of them is. Straight bars look like an average-fest of women on display compared to the creatures lurking in this dark basement.

They are undeniably some of the most beautiful women I have ever seen.

I walk inside and make my way to the center bar. The bartender is wearing a bright blue sequined dress that accentuates her cleavage, and legs that go on for days. She gives me a warm smile and asks what I would like to drink.

"Just a bottle of water, please," I respond.

"Taking it easy tonight?" she says in response. I give a nod of agreement as she hands me my water and tells me there will no charge. I make my way to a corner booth off the side of the dance floor. The walls here are plastered with famous female movie stars from the golden age of cinema; Betty Davis, Elizabeth Taylor, Audrey Hepburn, Lauren Bacall, Hedy Lamarr, Sophia Loren, Grace Kelly, Vivian Leigh, and of course, Marilyn Monroe.

Seated beneath Marilyn is a sweet looking girl all by herself. My heart is pounding, but she does not look too intimidating and I am here to meet someone so I just go for it.

"Hello, may I share your table," I said.

"Sure," she says quite plainly. Her eyes are a pristine shade of blue and she looks very out of place here. The greenness coming off of her is adorable. And adorable is not the type of woman I am looking for I need someone who can take charge. I think I may have made a horrible mistake sitting down.

"Is this your first time here," she asks after quite a few minutes of the two of us staring off into bar space.

"It is," I respond. "A friend recommended it to me as I never even knew it was here." A sweet laugh escapes her lips. "I know, most people have no idea it exists, but it does," she said.

I cannot get over just how wholesome she comes across. She is beautiful, that is certain, and the stiletto heels she is wearing are anything but innocent, but that could all just be a rouse.

I don't have much time so it's time to just be blunt and move on if I need to. This may be my first time, but I can manage getting to the point quickly and if I look like an ass. I can just run right out of here and never look back.

"I'm here because I am looking for a woman to join my husband and I in a threesome. We don't want to ask anyone we know, and we'd prefer a lesbian so she would be more inclined to pleasure me than him since he likes to watch. She also must be capable of taking orders and giving them as we play rough quite often," I blurted out.

She looked at me for a long moment. Her eyes burning into mine. Searching for an answer I could not provide.

"Come with me," she said as she stood up and outstretched her hand.

"Where to?" I asked.

"Just trust me," she answered.

It was hard not to trust someone who came across as such an angel as she so I did as I was told and followed her through the bar. She led me down a barely lit hallway. Lights were scattered every few feet or so on the walls but the shadows of light they returned were minimal at best.

We came to the end of the hall and she pushed aside a curtain to reveal one plush armchair, covered in purple velvet set inside a carved out semi-circle in the wall. To the right of the chair there were fur-covered manacles bolted into the wall and a stepping stool beneath them.

She pushed the stool aside and then pushed me up against the wall, as the curtain swung closed behind us and we were plunged into sudden darkness. Her hands moved up and down my body, caressing my breasts from behind, and she pushed herself up against me so I could feel the heat from her body radiating through my clothes as her hot breath was on my neck.

She took my left hand first and placed it in one of the manacles, closing it around me. I knew I could break free if I needed to, as it was not tight, but the excitement running through my veins at what may come next stopped me from stopping her plan. One hand cuffed above my head, against the cold brick wall, and she continued to caress every inch of me. With my back to her, I had no idea what to expect, could not see where she was headed, and did not dare ask.

Her mouth found its way to my ankles, and her tongue and teeth nipped at them like a playful cat. Her hands were on my thighs, kneading the flesh before she grabbed hold of the sides of my garter belt straps and played them like a guitar string.

The elastic snapped against my thighs; it was painful and delightful all at once. Working her way back up my body she bit my earlobe, and then my shoulder before grabbing my right arm and placing it in the other manacle. I was completely at her mercy now. A pawn to be taken advantage of any way she so desired.

My dress was pushed up to my waist and her fingers pushed inside of me with a great thrust. Deeper and deeper, faster and faster, she moved them. I was so wet I could feel myself dripping down my thighs. Her free hand spanked me, and spanked me again. Her fingers suddenly removed themselves from inside of me.

"Bend over as far as you can," she said in an alarming deep sexy voice. I obliged. Being cuffed did not make it easy but I bent as far as I could, my arms being stretched to the point of misery by the effort.

"Good girl," she said. "Now spread your legs wide."

Her hand glided down my backside, tickling me around the crack until suddenly she was not touching me any longer.

A moment passed, her breath now hot on my lower back, the steel tip of her stiletto picking up the small amount of light coming in under the curtain.

I watched her shoe like it was the most amazing thing I had ever seen as I waited for what was coming. I could feel every breath she took, her chest rising and falling against me.

Then it happened. In one quick thrust she put her entire fist inside of me. I was paralyzed in pain and pleasure all at the same time. The enormity of the size stretching by body beyond limits, and the sensations pulsing through me were immeasurable. Her other hand cupped by breast hard as she fisted me over and over again, each time deeper than the next.

I cried out as my body spasmed in an orgasmic display of absolute pleasure. She removed her hands from me and stepped back. I hung there, my legs too weak to support my entire body until she removed my hands from the manacles.

Turning to face her I said, "You are amazing."

She touched my cheek with the back of her hand and then turned away, pushing the curtain back and disappeared from my sight. I righted my clothes, and tried to make myself presentable as best I could in the dark. I returned to the bar and she was seated again in the corner, the same innocent look upon her face and her eyes shining with naiveté.

I knew the real truth behind the sweet smile and gentile manner. I took a slip of paper from inside of my purse and wrote my phone number down. No name, just the number, and handed it to her as I was leaving. She called two days later and told me she was interested. Now here we are, about to open the door and let in the unforgettable silver capped stiletto heels. I can barely contain my excitement.

~

"The Unforgettable Silver Capped Stilettos" (Part Three)

By Jessica Lucas

Time appeared to stand still after the knock on the door. My feet were planted in place, unable to move, and my mouth could not release a single word. I looked towards him, and saw the hesitation on his face. Could he be just as nervous as me?

Or was I imagining the entire thing so I could feel better about the fact that my mind was racing with anxiety and my body paralyzed out of fear, or excitement, or both mingled together in a perplexing state of emotions? It did not matter.

What we both wanted was behind the door, and we were not about to turn the opportunity away. What was the safe word again? I could not remember.

As I thought back to that night, shackled to a wall, bent over, with my legs spread open, and the extreme ecstasy that came later I urged my legs to move. Begged my mind to calm down and enjoy the moment, and for the life of me somehow I managed to make my way to the door. I turned the knob, swung the door open, and there she stood.

I had not remembered how tall she was. Her legs went on for what seemed like miles, and the teeny tiny tight red skirt she was wearing did not hide the fact. Her hair was pulled back in a loose bun, with tiny strands escaping around her temples and down over her shoulders. She was a sight to behold, with a soft shade of blush on her cheeks and ruby red lipstick. Her lips parted in a sweet angelic smile.

"What a tease," I thought to myself. I know better than to fall for the naive girl-next-door bit she plays all too well.

"Welcome," I blurted out a bit too loud.

The smile remained planted on her face as she said nothing in return and merely walked into the room. She had a bag over her shoulder that far too large to use as day purse. Oh, how I wondered what goodies were hiding in her bag. My desire to find out quickly squashed any nervousness I had felt before.

How he was doing at the moment I did not know, I'd nearly forgotten he was there but I'd never admit that to him. One glance down at her silver capped stilettos and I was ready for the night to continue. She made her way to the armchair by the fireplace and placed her bag down on the floor. Finally, she spoke to the both of us.

"Are you ready to get started?" she said matter-of-factly. I loved how she took charge without hesitation. She may be angelic looking but a tiny devil lives inside of her...a very playful devil.

"I'm Br..." he started to say before she cut him off abruptly.

"I don't need to know your name. I'm not here to chat, I'm here to see just how well the two of you take directions," she said as if she was leading an orchestra.

"Play me as much as you want," I thought. *"I am your instrument all night."*

The fear I thought I had seen on his face quickly faded away when she started giving orders.

"I want you to sit in the chair by the fireplace," she told him. "And take off your underwear, I want to see every inch of you."

He obliged, removing his underwear to reveal an already rock hard cock. It looked like it could burst at any second, but he knew better than to allow that to happen.

"Now, you and I are going to get on the bed," she told me.

Tiny butterflies jumped around in my stomach I was so electrified by just the idea of having her touch me again. I made my way over to the bed and sat down. I was quickly told that was not the position she wanted me in oh, how I loved to hear her reprimand me.

"Get on all fours, sideways to the end of the bed," she said. "Your ass in his direction."

I obliged because, I pride myself at being very good at following directions. I heard the zipper on her bag open but could not see what she was taking from it. A cough from his direction signaled it must be something good, and a tad surprising. The bed creaked as she climbed up behind me. I was on all fours, my ass to her face, as he waited patiently in his chair for more directions. I too was eager to find out what was in store for us when I felt it.

It was a gigantic thing between my legs, rubbing up against my pussy. The coldness sought out my heat like a moth to a flame. I peeked down between my legs to see exactly what it was, even though I knew what was happening.

The strap-on dildo must have been twelve inches long and four inches thick. It was colossal. The sight of it rubbing up against me, applying pressure that forced me to moan in ecstasy, quickly made it my favorite toy, ever.

It was all I could do to not beg her to put it inside of me. To let me feel myself wrapped around it while she thrusted it in-and-out of me repeatedly.

"Do you like this?" she asked him.

"Yes," he whispered.

"Louder," she nearly yelled.

"I like it, I like it," he answered.

"Good," she said. "I want to see your cock grow purple because it's so excited and wants to explode with giant geyser of cum all over itself."

I nearly exploded in laughter. I'd never have thought of that one, nor did I think he would ever oblige, but he did.

His hand moved to his shaft and started working magic on it. Up and down, fingers tightening and loosening as he went, his head tilted backwards from the enjoyment and his eyes began to close.

"No, keep your eyes open and on us," she demanded.

His eyes flew back open and that is when I felt it, all twelve inches. She grabbed me by the waist and thrust the dildo inside of me. All the way in it went, until I felt it hit the back of me, pressed up against my farthest barrier, and retreated again to repeat the motion over-and-over again. Oh, the immense pleasure.

My pussy was so wet I could see it dripping on the bed. I was nearly suffocating myself because I had forgotten to breathe due to the intense feelings soaring through my body. I glanced over at him and his eyes were glazed over with lasciviousness.

He wanted to participate, I could tell, but would she let him? She would.

"Get up and get behind me," she told him.

"I want you to stick that hard cock of yours as deep inside of me as you possibly can. When you think you can't go any further, go further."

"Oh, this is fantastic," I thought, between moans and the occasional moment of near-unconsciousness. I was floating weightless it seemed, my body being devoured by extreme satisfaction with every thrust and pullback she managed.

When his cock entered her she gave out a slight moan.

"So she likes being taken, too, does she?" I thought to myself with a grin. Her body slumped down on my back, her firm breasts pressed into my

flesh, and her hands came around me to grab my breasts. My nipples were rock hard, and I hadn't noticed how long they had been that way. The dildo was still inside of me, but she was not moving. Instead, she was playing with my hard nipples; pulling on them, pinching gently and then with a bit more force, before she cupped both breasts and massaged them equally. Her thumbs kept riding over me in quick soft grazing movements.

The feel of the dildo inside of me, between my legs, still pushing on my insides, still making me grow wetter with every moment, combined with the teasing of my breasts made we want to scream.

I could see his legs behind her and every time he pushed inside of her, gave her every inch of that gorgeous cock of his; she bumped up against me, and the dildo made its way in-and-out of me. We were like a sex train combined of his cock, the dildo, and my pussy, with two breasts leading the charge. Our "train" continued for a while before her hands moved from my breasts and she gave the word for a shift change.

Instead of telling him to stop she reached around him and slapped his ass. The groan he gave was no signal that he meant to stop, but when she did it again he took more notice.

He removed his cock from her and she took the dildo out of me, but not before giving me one last big thrust. She instructed him to sit on the bed with his legs crossed in front of me. I was to remain on all fours. "Suck his cock," she said.

"*Happily*," I thought. The minute my mouth touched him it was not the feel of his extreme rigidness that made me nearly cum right then and there, or the sound of the deep groan that escaped his lips when I took every inch of him inside of me. It was something else. It was the taste of *her* on his cock that excited me.

"I want to see his cock in your throat," she said.

She scooted her way underneath me and I stiffened with anticipation. I knew once she was between my legs I should expect the unexpected. But she kept her fist to herself, and gave me the pleasure of her tongue with a little help from another special toy she had pulled out of her bag. It looked like a tongue depressor, but covered in little hard rounded plastic balls.

The minute her tongue touched me I was in heaven; the second she added the toy to the mix by tickling my clot with it I refused to hold back any longer. With his cock down my throat, my lips covered in her nectar, I let myself go. I moaned and screamed, sending the waves from my vocal cords down his cock. His entire body twitched as it was too much for him to handle, and he came in my mouth, the cum coating the back of my throat.

My entire body was tingling. I gave his cock one last deep up and down movement, my tongue pushing against it to hit his favorite spot beneath the knob, before I pulled my mouth from him. She still lay beneath me, but she had stopped moving her tongue or playing with her toy. I could feel how swollen my pussy must be. How wet and hot it must feel to the touch.

Just as I was getting out from on top of her, she stopped me. She grabbed my hips and tilted me down onto her face. Her tongue made one last long lick from top to bottom. She touched every spot; hit every crevice, before she stopped.

It seemed the taste of me was something she could not get enough of either.

Author: Laney Oden

*Laney Oden, gypsy, sex fiend, and a hopeless
romantic all wrapped into one. She considers herself a
"Princess of all trades." When she isn't writing you will
catch her playing: on the beach, in the water, or in her
bed. She's tough to love and hard to handle, but once
you get a little, there's not enough time in the day to
get enough. She's a tough one to crack but once you do,
she will give you all she's got.*

"Horny and Stuck in My Car"
By Laney Oden

Downtown Seattle is a cluster fuck around
this time at night. The constant honking of car horns,
pedestrians making plans about after work drinking,
and professionals already settling at the bars after a
long day of bullshit. Thank God it's Friday.

It's 5:30 pm. He watches nearby as she makes
her way to her car. She's so sexy with those long
thighs that make him lose his breath, for an instant.
Her pencil skirt was beautifully framing her amazing
curves. His mind wanders as he anticipates that his
wife will home shortly.

"Can you?" She sounds just the way she
looks; exotic, sexy, and aiming to please his every
need. He loves the rush that she gives him.

"She's almost home," he exclaims," you know
it's a risk."

"Come fuck me baby. I need you right now."
His dick is solid. He is compelled to go to her, but his
wife will be home any minute. He walks out of the
shadows towards the unlit parking lot.

Her mind is racing. Her body tingles as she
know what's about to happen. It's been nearly a year
that they've seen each other almost everyday at this

time. She has the sex drive of a teen that just learned what fornication was all about.

She can't stop masturbating to the thought of anything that walks with a hard-on. She needs her fix and his dick game is always on point. She's beyond horny and as she takes her bra off in anticipation when there is a tap on her window.

She clicks open the door lock without even looking at who it is. He slides in the passenger seat next to her. He reaches out to her and aggressively pulls her to him. She lets out a slight moan.

"Mmm baby, I've been waiting for your cock all day," she says as she reaches down and grabs his erection. "He seems to have missed me too."

Their kissing is fast and fun. His cell rings.

He continues to slip his palm onto her pussy. It's soft, warm, and open for him. The cell keeps buzzing. She's shocked when he enters two of his fingers, but her mouth doesn't produce any words as he takes his other hand and puts it up to his mouth as a 'shh, don't say anything' sign.

He continues finger fucking the shit out of her, while she stays quiet.

"Honey, I'm home. Where are you? We have plans at 6:15," says a female voice on the other end.

"Yes. I know... I'm coming as fast as I can." He pushes the red button and the phone goes dark.

He takes his hand out of her and motions her to the back seat. She's on fire. He spreads her legs as he pulls her panties off. He looks at her for what seems like an eternity. She moans, wanting him. She's dripping wet. His face gets close to her pussy. He kisses her inner thighs, then runs his tongue close to her cunt. His mouth falls on her opening and he sucks on her lips, his tongue deep in her.

She lets out a sigh.

"Oh my god! I want you to fuck me like you

mean it baby! Please fuck me hard!" She begs.
He smiles." You want it?" He pulls her to him.

She screams with delight as he enters her wet
and tight pussy.

"Faster, baby. Oh you feel so good, don't stop."
Her breasts are perfect. He licks each nipple, as they
get harder than they have ever been.

He bites them. She lets out deeps sounds as
he pushes deeper into her. Moan by moan he takes
everything. On and on she takes him. She rubs her
clit as he touches her insides with his cock.

He flips her over, taking her from behind. He's
lying on top of her while she continues to rock her
body back and forth. She doesn't care if anybody
happens to see them fucking in the back seat of her
car.

Her body trembles. She nears her peak and
his body radiates with her climax. All at once, their
bodies collide. Full force. She explodes in orgasm.

His eyes open. He grabs his phone out of his
pocket, suddenly nervous. 7:12pm. Fuck. Fuck.
Fuck! Three missed calls and two voicemails. She sits
upright next to him.

"You," she smiles, "you just know."
She kisses his lips. She kisses down his face to his
chest, across his midsection, his pelvic area.

She takes his solidness and puts it in her
mouth. Her tongue strokes up and down and all
around his cock. He looks down at her with lush eyes.
His body feeds on her every move. Her tongue makes
him grow even bigger. He knows this is wrong but he
doesn't stop her. She sits up and wraps a leg across
his lap as she whispers in his ear.

"Put it in. I'm going to ride until you cum, but
before you cum, let me know.

I want to taste you again."
He listens to her request. She feels so warm.

They kiss intimately. She wants this night to go on...and on...and on.

He thinks to himself that his body is on the verge. "I'm about to cum. Oh babyyyy." She hops off and sticks his cock into her mouth just as he shoots his wad deep in the back of her throat. She loves it. It thrills her to please him to this extent. She swallows everything. He tastes good.

"I've got to go," she tells him. He doesn't want her to leave. He wants to make his way back inside her. He wants to love her body more and more. She dresses.

He touches her, this time harder, as he grabs her hair and yanks her head back, biting her neck. She whimpers a little.

"Until next time," he whispers to her.

He gets out of the car and walks away, gets on his cell and makes a call.

~

Author: J.P. Georges

J.P. Georges was born in the wrong time. She loves bodices, boots, leather and lace, and finds herself often daydreaming of previous eras. Whether her stories are true, she cannot really say, but she does not deny the ability to regress into several past incarnations in the attempts of reuniting with her past lovers.

"Ever So Much Fun"
Author: J.P. Georges

It is 1925 Los Angeles. We call it the "Roaring Twenties" for a reason. The city is filled with a mixture of new arrivals like Chinese laborers, Armenian carpet sellers and Jewish families living next door to wannabe silent filmmakers and businessmen.

The blend of culture and customs provides a colorful and dynamic human landscape during the day. At night, it becomes downright devilish.

After the carpet sellers roll 'em up and families tuck the children to bed, the flappers and Dapper Dan's come out to play.

Grateful to the fashion Gods, we now sport swell dresses above the knee, with plenty of length of gams showing in back-seamed stockings.

Some gals go brassiere-less. It's a final "so long" to the Victorian elite who clipped their corset strings after the Century turned the corner.

I cut my below-the-shoulder hair to a short pixie, a popular look
that can also sometimes secretly help one double as the male gender. I like to play with traditional roles, and found one particular speakeasy that on Friday nights cater to a woman only crowd, though at times I could swear that a few men sneak in the

masqueraders do such a grand job at disguise.

Up until a few nights ago, I had never had sex with a female, but had been winding myself up like a top ready to spin.

I hung back up my three tiered fringed ruby colored dress that I had pulled out and dismissed the black stockings, when I asked myself aloud, *"why don't I go as a man tonight?"* The thought itself was so provocative that I was getting moist between my legs. Walking downtown in a three-piece suit and spats on my shoes, my hair slicked back and my panties stuffed with...geez Louise, what would I stuff my panties with?

I rolled up a stocking and wadded it near my crotch but it felt too light, not enough pressure or weight to truly be a man's pride.

Looking around my room, I found a few objects that were in question: a perfume bottle, a hand mirror, an eight-inch high wooden Art Deco duck. None of these seemed very forgiving.

At the side of my bed on the end table was a periodical novelette of Pierre Louys' Chanson de Bilitis, a racy compilation of poems depicting debauchery from the Isle of Lesbos and beyond. Basically, it was my education towards the taboo of sexual self exploration and the ultimate erotica: a journey into the sensational promise land of a woman's flowered petals in the quest to bring her to ecstasy.

I realized that before I could possibly know how to touch another woman, I would need to please myself. I would often read while I used a variety of objects to insert and rub against myself and often I would watch myself with my hand mirror in fascination to see the creamy substance push out of me.

Tonight was no exception. I lay back on my

bed, wearing only my peach satin nightgown, my panties now on the floor. I decided to try something new. No gadgets, no objects, just my fingers exploring myself like I would another person.

I opened the novelette by fanning the pages and stopping mid book and began to read a page of this Belgium writer's description of the elusive mound of virgin delight pursued by a raving beast of a huntress who would not let off the hunt until she devoured it.

"Her tongue," he wrote, "licked and slapped upon the prey that was tied up against a tree with her dress ripped apart. The young dear was helpless as the huntress-beast woman ravished her with her tongue, teeth and lips between the moaning and trapped girls legs, inserting a finger and pulling it out, smelling her essence and replacing two more, deep inside the girl, the huntress pushed in and out, her mouth on top of the girl's until she betrayed herself and felt pleasure."

I pretended to be the girl in my mind and then changed into the huntress. I brought myself to a point of nearly releasing my pent up energy when I put the novelette down.

I must play the part tonight; I must be the man. I wanted to feel the power of my thrust and my weight on top, I wanted to insert my fingers deep inside and lick and suck until she exploded in my mouth. Wet and ready, I slicked my black hair back and parted it on the side.

Five foot eleven inches, small breasted and long-legged, I cut quite a male figure, an intoxicating androgen, a delicious somewhere between male and female. I grabbed my cigarillos and the last touch: a rolled up novelette stuffed in my trousers.

I hired a car to get downtown, the driver all the way uncomfortable of what to call me.

We arrived at our destination fifteen minutes later, a black door without a sign about a block from the LA Times building. He realized it then.

When I was leaving he leaned over and said, " If you don't find what you want tonight honey, take a look at this," and he unzipped the front of his trousers to show me a circumcised penis about six and a half inches in length. Seeing this, I knew him to be Jewish. I smiled and closed the door.

At the entrance to the secret speakeasy was a mountain of a bruiser. I nodded at him at the same time two chippies trotted up.

The doorman opened it for us and I went in, feeling alive and excited. The smoky room, dark in the corners, was filled with wall-to-wall dancers, partygoers, dames, fops and flappers. The green liquid of absinthe in the hands of several bar leaner's, a back area of opium smokers and an overall air of wildness and wonder spurred on into frenzied floor dancers at the Charleston.

The four-piece all female band dressed in tuxedos was playing a rousing rendition of *"Ain't We Got Fun."* The whole joint looked like people were having just that: more fun than they ever had in their life. Then, I saw her.

My cigarillo lit, I checked my pocket watch and determined that at midnight I would be between the Sheba's gams. It was eleven forty-five and I knew I would have to work fast. I ordered a whisky sour to give me some liquid courage. Thankful for these joints illegally operating in the time of Prohibition, only gave me extra feelings of excitement. The thrill of being caught, and then worse, dressed as a man, turned me on like a radio at full blast.

She was beautiful: a petite blonde with eyes that showed a mixture of demureness and vixen. A small button nose and round cheeks, perky breasts and a wicked smile. A she-devil in angel's clothing. I approached, glass in hand. I introduced myself and she grabbed my hand.

Without a word, she pulled me into a dark corner booth. She closed the curtain. Her lips, bright red and perfectly lined like a cupie-doll, were whispering in my ear. I couldn't hear a word, but felt a twinge in my stomach.

She rubbed my leg with a gloved hand, giggling and then moved midway and felt the rolled up novelette between them. Her eyes went wide and she looked perplexed. She removed her glove and slipped her fingers under my vest and white silk short and felt my nipples. Relieved, she twisted one of them, hard. I inhaled sharply.

"You tried to fool me!" she laughed and kept moving from my right to left breast, turning and twisting. The pain felt magnificent. I stared at her red lips and parted them with a finger.

I inserted a finger into her mouth, my lips close to her and said, "How would you like these somewhere else?"

She let out a groan. I was wet with anticipation, I knew this was it, the moment; this would be my fantasy come true. I reached down and lifted her dress, feeling the garter holding up her pink stockings, like the boyfriends had done to me.

I was surprisingly good at this- the gender pretender in the male role, it felt...natural.

My heart beating faster, I slowly kneaded her inner thighs, each motion creeping closer to her sex. Her lips parted, her breaths were coming in loud panting sounds. She suddenly grabbed my hand and placed it on her panties. I gasped. She was soaking wet. I lost my sense of logic, fear, and politeness.

I pulled her dress up, turned her towards me, yanked her out of the booth and picked her up. I couldn't believe my own strength. I set her down on the table and spread her legs apart. In the dimly lit corner, I could see parts of her, her sex organ, her opening. I stared, my mouth watering.

She watched me as I slowly went in with one finger, and then two. I moved to the rhythm of the music playing in the front room.

The band was singing, *"in the daytime, in the evening... ain't we got fun?"* She whispered as if answering, "So much fun..." as I was now inserting a tongue into her. I rapidly moved my it over her, in her, biting her inner thighs, going back to her sex and lapping up her juices.

Then I climbed on top of her and shoved my tongue into her mouth, French style. She arched her back and I placed an arm around it, lifting her to me. There were shouts from the other room.

Someone yelling, "The fuzz is here!" Women were screaming and I heard them running. Glass broke and the band stopped. The paddy wagons pulled up with sirens and crashed through the back door. I froze.

"Shhh," said the gal and we quietly went under the table. She giggled a little and pulled out a reefer from her purse.

"What are you doing? The police are here!" I whispered.

"I know," she said, isn't this exciting?"

She lit up and gave me a puff. I never had anything like it. My head spun a bit, I felt giddy. As mayhem was going on in the front rooms, we were under the table heavy petting and getting loaded.

Her legs were wrapped around mine and she asked me to remove my slacks so she could see what the bulge really was. When I pulled out the novelette and started reading her erotica in French, she placed her hand on her sex. It made my skin hot watching her.

I heard the policemen making arrests.
My heart was beating out of my chest. She asked me
to please her before the handcuffs were on us.

She sat back on the booth seat and spread
her legs, showing herself up close as I stayed under
the table. I resumed my tongue in her, licking faster
and faster as I heard footsteps in the hallway near us.
There were men's voices getting closer.

I inserted two fingers, then three as I kept my
mouth on her quivering rosebud, round and round,
in and out, gently grabbing with my teeth, then
feeling her with my fingers. She was moaning,
moving, wet. The two officers pulled back the curtain
just as she was exploding with pleasure into my
mouth.

I sheepishly came out from underneath the
table, wiping my face with my ascot. The policemen's
eyes went wide as saucers, putting it all together.

We were piled in the paddy and off we went to
precinct, to spend the night in a holding cell with
forty other gals and getting booked for participating
in liquor usage and other illegal activities.

In the morning they let us go after we paid a
five spot fine, but the dame didn't have it so I paid for
her too; not a bad trade off for a night of ever so
much fun.

~

"Lady of the Manor"
By J. P. Georges

Sweat formed on his neck as he moved faster and faster. His heart was pumping hard, his muscles strong and athletic, as she was on top of him, in sync, balanced, and squeezing her legs at his sides to go harder still. His nostrils widened to suck up more air, his back tensed, breathing became faster as his rib cage blew in and out. He strained to go on. He was dripping wet from the exertion, but he loved to run, loved to dig his legs into the earth like he was flying. She pulled him up by sitting back, releasing her leg pressure and lengthening the reins.

His gait home was like a little jig, somewhere between a walk and a trot, head high in the air, ears pricked forward, tail slightly raised; he was a Thoroughbred after all. Both horse and rider like one being they pranced towards the stables near her manor home.

The gray skies darkened as they approached the yard, and she was concerned for his well being since he was still too hot to be put away in his stall.

She called out for the new groom but there was no answer. Irritated, she dismounted and led her horse into the barn. She was accustomed to taking care of her own horses since she was a child, even if they always had hired help, and since she rode astride and threw away the conventions of the side saddle, she never needed anyone to help her on or off her mounts. Today though, she would have liked some help. In opposition to her families many wishes, she also rode in breeches, a fashion not quite caught on in these Victorian times laden with regulations on what it meant to be a lady in high society.

Her horse's breath started to slow and he chomped on his bit as she led him towards the tack room to unsaddle. The indoor barn smelled of the straw bedding, leather, and horses; an earthy and specific combination that she loved.

She tried to get her father to bottle it, saying that wherever she went, she would like to have the unique smell of a horse stable with her. He of course, thought her mad and silly, and dismissed the idea. Though girls who love horses know that she meant it.

She threw her quip into the tack room and looked around for her horse's halter. Suddenly, the new groom stepped out of the tack room, shirt unbuttoned, hair disheveled, and trousers askew, in long socks sans boots. Her horse shied and snorted. She pulled him back, only to stare at the magnificent bare chest in front of her. He couldn't be much older than herself she thought, twenty-three, twenty-four, at the most.

His skin was a bit darker and more olive complexioned that the usual pale white faces of Derbyshire that she grew up with, or that her father employed, even the laborers and stablemen. The sun simply made a rare appearance in this part of the world.

He blinked a few times and brushed back his black thick hair with one hand. He had clearly been asleep.

"Milady," he said sheepishly, "Please, may I take Barnaby, miss?" She gave him a crooked smile. He seemed shy, reserved. She thought he might be too easy.

"What, with no boots on? Clearly, you've never known the weight of one hundred stone landing on your toes."

He looked down, and realized his lack of dress. He hurried back into the tack room, and pulling on his boots, buttoning his shirt in hopping unison, her grabbed Barnaby's reins and led him towards the stall. She watched him coordinate himself as the hind end of her horse ambled down the brick walkway.

They disappeared in the stall together, and she stretched her neck to try and see them above the partition walls that divided each horse. He went to work untacking the horse, currying and brushing him. Barnaby nod his head up and down, liking the feeling of being groomed. A towel lay nearby that he used to dry off Barnaby's wet net, shoulders, and areas that had lathered.

She walked slowly towards the stall. The groom was bent over, cleaning a hoof with the pick, his backside towards her.

He cut such a nicely shaped figure of a male, she thought. Just as she thought it, she felt guilty for *not* feeling guilty. She was told a young lady was supposed to feel a certain way about things, in 1889.

"You must be James," she said, startling him. She laughed when he jumped. "You're more spooky than my horse."

"You've caught me with me pants down, nearly, " he replied in his thick Irish brogue.

"Yes," she said, looking a little displeased.

"I'm...I'm sorry miss." He completed cleaning the horse's feet and dropped the pick into a wooden tack box. He patted the horse on his cheek and the horse rubbed his head against James's shoulder. Outside, the sound of rain came down.

"Good that you came back when you did, miss," he said, sneaking a look at her shape in the riding breeches. She looked outside through an open stall window.

"Yes," she said as the skies opened up and it started to pour. "Looks like I'll have to wait it out a bit before I get to the house. Unless of course you have a parasol?"

He looked around, and smiling answered,
"No, I'm afraid I don't." They stared at each other for a moment just a little too long to be polite.

She could feel her loins getting hot as her cheeks flushed. His bright blue eyes seemed to be looking right into her. A strand of air fell across one, he pushed it back in place.

"What area of Ireland are you from?" she asked, looking for conversation, looking to prolong their time together. Had she ever seen a man's body so perfect in its structure? She thought how much he reminder her of Barnaby strong muscled, big chested, handsome face, light brown skin and black hair, the same color as her horses forelock.

There was something different about him, something almost...wild. Like the Arabian ancestors her Thoroughbred has.

"I'm from Cork, but my people on my mothers side were Basque." *Ah,* she thought, *gypsies.*

He's was what was called a "traveler," an Irishman who grew up around horses in a nomadic horse culture that originally came from Romania, France, and other European back areas.

She inhaled. Was it he that she smelled in the mix of the stables, a deep musk, a strong pull on her senses? Her thighs trembled a little and she felt herself getting moist between her legs.

She was not a virgin, as she had known a man before. A cad, who in his promises, left her a month before the wedding day but not before he tasted the goods. He had hurt her in doing so, and she found herself not riding for almost half a year, until one day she decided to take back her power and doff the dress and sidesaddle and mount a horse, riding like a man, and fly across the countryside. There was no other feeling like it, she surmised, except maybe like the time of the present.

James must have sensed something from her, because he stepped forward to her, defying the rules of status between them. He was two feet away from her and she flushed. She could see his breath rising and falling underneath his shirt.

"I am the lady of the manor," she said, trying to cover up a slightly shaking voice, "And since my mother fell ill, I have been the person who manages all of my father's household when he is away. Myself, and his first houseman, of course."

The Irishman continued his stare. "Yes, mum," he said. He took a pause and turned again to the horse, untying the lead rope and removing his halter, He grabbed the tack box and excused himself and walked back to the tack room. She looked outside. The rain had not let up.

She called after him, "Where are Hobson and Flint today?"

He answered, coming out the tack room door, "In town mum, they needed supplies to finish the broken boards that the stallion took down last week."

She knew now they were alone and would be for hours, town was a long carriage ride off. Her heart beat faster. The rain came down even harder and louder. A few horses paced in their stalls while the hail pounded on the roof. A strong wind blew through the barn and the top stall doors swung open and closed. A few horses whinnied. Lightening flashed then loud thunder roared. She jumped and let out a small gasp.

James braved the storm and closed all the top stall doors from the outside. A few minutes later he returned soaked, and pulled the heavy main stable doors closed by dropping a four-foot board into two steel brackets.

It was quieter and the horses calmed down.
Some returned to their hay. She looked at him,
dripping on the bricks.

"You need to get out of those clothes," she
said, almost too quickly. He walked into the tack
room and looked about amidst the saddles and horse
blankets, but found nothing that would fit a human
form. He pulled his shirt off, revealing sculpted
muscles and a tight stomach, his chest perfectly
shaped. The lines of his shoulders into his back were
those like a statue of a Greek God, she thought as
she stood in the doorway.

He dropped his pants. She could see that he
was shivering from the cold even in the dimly lantern
lit room. He had no under garments to remove except
socks, which he pulled and wrung out in a bucket
against the tack room wall near where the bridles
hung. She sensed that he would turn at any moment,
and not knowing that she had been standing in the
doorway this whole time watching him undress, he
may shy again, and she would lose her opportunity.
Instead, she entered the room and closed the door
behind her. He turned at the noise.

There he stood, naked and cold, a God of a
man, so perfect in shape that she could not turn
away. His uncut member hung between his strong
thighs, and when he saw her look at it, it grew hard.
She gasped and took a step backward, making her
knees go out as she sat down upon a large trunk.

He slowly walked to her, no longer cold but
heated with the thought of having sex with the lady
of the house. He knew he could be let go, and even
worse, imprisoned, or maybe hung by a rope.

The danger of it excited him more and his eyes
blazed into hers as her approached. In front of her
now, he tentatively untied her stock tie and placed in

on the trunk next to her. He then turned her slightly
and removed the back lace from her corset.

She could smell his essence and it aroused
her. She reached out to touch him and he grabbed
her hand, a little rough, but then again he was not
the high society refined type of gent she was used to.

He placed her hand in his hardness and she
trembled, not letting go. A look came over his eyes
she hadn't seen in him before. It was a look she had
seen the stallions get before they were about to
mount ne of the broodmares. He took two or three
horse rugs and lay them on the floor of the tack room.

Then, picking her up in his arms, all the
whole looking at her, he laid her on them. He stood
above her, looking down, forcing her to see all of him,
to look up at him, as if he was higher status, as if he
was royalty, as if he could and would do anything to
her and she could not complain.

Her breathing became rapid. She wondered
what he would do as he stood above her. Slowly he
lowered his naked body onto hers. He straddled her
and suddenly without warning ripped open her silk
shirt, buttons scattering every which way. He stared
with penetrating eyes at her breasts, his mouth
hungry for them.

He tugged on her breeches and almost angrily
pulled them off. He then removed her silk stockings
and briefs. He stood above her again. She felt self-
conscious for a moment wondering what she was
doing here, and if he would now just abandon her in
this vulnerable state. A young attractive Victorian
lady lying on horse blankets with only an open shirt
as clothing. But instead he said nothing and lowered
himself near her.

He was on his knees and he grabbed both
ankles and pulled apart her legs so they went wide.

,

He had a good view of her; *a pretty, young, rich and very wet cunt,* he thought.

Without a word he did something to her she had never experienced. He placed his mouth on the most delicate of her petals, and inserted his tongue into her opening like she had heard about women doing that to each other in harems of the Orient, but that she had never assumed to be real, only fantasies. Instantly she arched her back and moaned.

His tongue licked and sucked her, all around her. He bit her inner things. She screamed.

He placed fingers in her mouth and mounted her. He made her legs stay s wide as he entered her. He then fucked her so hard and so deep that she thought she might be split in two.

Suddenly he pulled himself out and pinching one of her nipples, he stood up again, walked to the tack trunk and sat, watching her writhe and moan and wonder. He lit a cigarette, enjoying the fact that he had her, he was in control and he was above her. She begged him to make love to her. She moaned and moved, gyrating on the blankets.

"Put your fingers inside yourself and show me how much you want me," he commanded.

She did, at first using only one and then getting more confident, a second one. He found a riding crop with a wooden handle that twisted slightly. Pulled her hand away from herself and looked closely at her now wet sex.

He spread her lips with his fingers. She kept herself open wide. He picked up her legs and put her ankles on his shoulders. He leaned down to see her closely and inserted the wooden handle into her tight wet hole. She was scared but excited and he was hard, his cock pushed up against his stomach.

He had a big straight stiff one, as he watched the handle move in and out. He pulled it out completely and turned her over, her ass near his balls. He opened up her cheeks to see both holes. He pulled her forcibly to him, her ass high in the air as she rested on her elbows.

She felt vulnerable, but she could not stop him. She did not want to. He licked her everywhere, from ass to pussy, and when she felt as if she would cum, he would stop completely and do nothing. He played her.

"Beg." He said. "I want you to beg me to fuck you... milady. Your stable boy, taking you on the floor of the tack room." She was angered.

He wanted to humiliate her. She started to rise but he grabbed her, flipped her around and pressed his weight on her. He kissed her mouth, his tongue searching for hers. She melted.

He knew he had her. He found the stock tie on the trunk and tied her wrists, taking her arms above her head. "Beg me." he said again in the Irish lilt.

He lay on her, touching her softly now, and then suddenly hard, pinching her nipples, grabbing her breasts, putting a finger into her mouth and then lightly licking her thighs. He was all over her until she was moaning, moving and in exquisite torture.

"Please, fuck me," she finally let out in a moaning desire. "What was that, I couldn't quite hear you," he said, knowing full well that what she had asked him. "Please, fuck me, please, I beg you! Fuck me!"

He inserted himself into her and pumped her hard, moving in and out, almost pulling out, seeing the head of his cock at the edge of her little cunt and then pushing back in.

He started to sweat and fell onto her. His rhythm slowed as he placed a hand over her two tied ones and his mouth met hers and he found that inner spot with is cock.

She exploded on him, cumming on him, shaking with him and he pulled himself out and let looses all over her belly, breasts and then placed himself in her mouth for the very last of it. She nearly gagged as he forced himself into her, even though his hardness was leaving. He was so much man.

After several moments, he untied her wrists. He put on his wet clothes as she dressed into her dry yet scattered ones. He turned his back to her.

"I am the lady of the manor," she said, almost tearing up "and you will not turn your back to me."

He took a short pause before turning. She had never had a man look at her this way; like a wolf was hunting her.

"No, milady," he said, "no, I will not, my apologies." And he kissed her hard and held her close to him.

The rain subsided. She left the stable and walked to the house, unescorted. He unlatched all the top doors, letting in the crisp air. He watched her in the distance as she ascended the stairs to the manor house. She disappeared as the butler let her in. He returned to his duties and started mucking the first stall where the stallion resided.

Out the stall window he could see a familiar work wagon approaching with supplies.

~

Couples Interactive guide:

Record An Erotic Story For Your Sweetheart

There are many ways to show someone how much you desire them, and RawrWoman has created a very special treat for those who want to personalize their steamy message.

Use one of the unique love letters we have created and record it in your voice as a gift to your beloved. Put emphasis on the words and phrases that excite you most, and add a touch of your desire by throwing in a moan or two of your own, if you please.

Choose one of the following stories, hit record on your phone or computer, and prepare to have your lover yearning for your touch.

Come. Let's get started...

1.Her Story to Him   "Thinking Of You While Away"

2.His Story to Her   "A Sexy Love Letter"

3.Her Story to Her   "The Soft Satiny Feel Of Your Touch"

~

Her Story to Him
"A Sexy Love Letter"
By Skyler Knightley

Hey babe! You're all I've been able to think about since you left. Every night so I can dream of you, I've been putting on your favorite shirt so I can feel like you're arms are around me.

The smell of your amazing cologne mixed with the intoxicating scent all your own absolutely turns me on and is so comforting with you being so far away. I've been planning the perfect getaway for when you get back. I know how much you love the beach so I thought nothing would be better than an island escape. I imagine a secluded chateau that opens out onto our own private beach. I'm wearing your favorite dress with no panties so you can easily access what you've been denied for so long.

We have dinner reservations but we have other things in mind. I'm looking out at the miraculous view and you wrap your arms around me from behind.

I inhale deeply capturing all those smells from your favorite shirt that I used for comfort while you were gone. You lean into me with your breath dancing across my neck. I stretch back so I can feel even closer to you.

You slowly kiss the pulse point on my neck as the sun sinks into the water. I reach my arms back and drape them softly around your neck. Your hands slowly travel to my breasts where you imitate the rhythm with your hands that your lips are doing to my neck.

My lips gently part as my breath catches from you teasing my nipples through the fabric of my dress. You pull my dress over my head and toss it aside without a thought. You lightly place my own hands on my breasts with yours on top.

You help me find the rhythm that you were caressing my breasts with earlier. You move your hands to my waist and peak over my shoulder so you can see me pull gently at my nipples.

I know you love to watch me touch myself so the sensation mixed with that notion makes me cry out in ecstasy. Your hands little by little make their way to my throbbing clit.

Your index finger deliberately caresses my opening and a smile crosses your face because I am so wet for you. You pluck your finger into your mouth to get a taste of the sensation that you have been missing for so long. A slight groan escapes your lips because you love so much how I taste.

Suddenly you throw me down on the bed face up. You sensuously remove my high heels and lay a kiss on top of each of my feet. Your eyes are smoky with desire so I arch my back and spread my legs wide so you can see exactly what you want.

You lick your lips longingly as you stare at my dripping clit. You come to rest between my legs, placing your finger on top of my throbbing button. You rub it leisurely in circles watching my response intently. As the passion begins to rise, you plunge your finger deep into my wetness.

I gasp out at the abrupt, astounding phenomenon. You withdraw bit by bit making me fight to grab a breath. You grab my hand, pull me into you, and then turn me around. Your finger once again finds my pulsating clit and begins to move it back and forth.

I collapse into you almost unable to be on my knees from the shaking sensation coursing through my body. You change the rhythm to up and down causing me to crumple onto all fours with my fine ass facing toward you. You slide your hands onto both my ass cheeks and gently squeeze.

Your left hand gives me a swift spank while I hear you unzipping your pants. I feel you slowly rub your massively, hard dick against my throbbing clit. You find my soaked opening and plunge in deep.

I am absolutely taken aback as you fill me absolutely and completely. Your rhythm is hard and quick causing my body to shake and quake with absolute nirvana. There is nothing more that I love than you driving into me with absolute abandon.

I feel the orgasm begin to rise as you pound harder. We collapse onto the bed in simultaneous bliss, vibrating from the utter pleasure we've just experienced together. We roll over into each other's arms, trading kisses that twist between soft and passionate.

I gently push you onto your back and straddle you. Your thumbs drift up to my nipples, refusing to let them be anything but hard. Your incredible teasing is causing me to get wet all over again.

I glance down and see you extremely stiff with perfect desire. I lean over, giving you a wicked grin, and pluck your flawless dick between my puckered, sultry lips. I melt down the shaft with my mouth and lick up with my long tongue. When I reach the head, I slightly suck then lick it before dissolving back down, taking in every inch of you completely and utterly.

I can feel the taste of you slip down the back of my throat and I suck faster wanting more to escape. My tempo quickens as I feel you grow longer and harder but when I reach your glorious head; I work slowly licking every part of it.

I notice your tight balls and make my tongue dance over them, slightly sucking before returning to your vast dick. I melt back down, I feel you brace and explode down my throat.

I swallow enjoying you coming so much into me.

When I pluck your cock free, I look into your desired filled eyes and smile. I plant an incredible kiss on your perfect lips. I straddle you so I can feel the warmth emanating off your body.

I love how you always make me feel warm in so many ways. There's no one else who I want inside me or to make me cum so hard. You're the only one who can make me feel completely and utterly sexy to the core.

I've missed you for so long and this moment in our absolute paradise is everything I wanted it to be. I can't wait to tell you about the next day in our Eden where I break out the handcuffs and the day after that when we have sex on the beach.

I need you and I'll feel absolutely crazy with longing until you return. I kept my promise and have stayed away from my vibrator so I will be ready and willing to make you satisfied for endless hours. See you soon, babe. I'm counting the days.

~

His story to Her:

"Thinking Of You While Away From Home"
By, Jacob Summers

Lover... each night I am gone, and every morning when I wake up this is what I will imagine I am doing to your body.

"You ready, baby?"

I think you're wearing far too many clothes. How about we take off your blouse. Lift your arms up. Yes, I want to see your sexy stomach and creamy skin. You're so sexy baby, and the line of your torso, near your rib cage drives me wild. The way it curves into your waist. Now your bra; toss it on the floor. Yes, show me your perfect breasts. I love how they bounce when you laugh.

I'm already growing hard and I've not even touched you yet. Now how about we get rid of that skirt? And the panties, too. Show me your seductive body. I can see every inch of you now, and you're beautiful. Your allure is intoxicating. Lay down on the bed so I can pleasure every inch of you. I've got my hands around your waist. My tongue is toying with the skin around your navel.

I'm on my knees to you, devouring every inch of your stomach with my tongue. Small, little circles I'm making with my hot mouth against your cool skin.

You like that don't you?

But there is more, of course. Your beautiful full breasts are moving up and down with your hard breath. How about I place one of your nipples in my mouth. I can tell from your moan that you like it.

I'm suckling your nipple. It is so hard in my mouth; my teeth can't help but nibble a tiny bit.

Oh, you want more pressure do you? And my tongue? Yes, my tongue is flicking against your nipple now. I love how your back arches with each touch. I can feel just how hot this is making you. I'm moving on to your other breast now. My hand has found its way to your pussy; your hot, wet pussy.

My fingers are playing with you now, my palm applying pressure as they move inside of you. Your pussy is so soft and wet. My mouth continues to devour your breast. Kissing the edges, my teeth pulling at your nipple.

I've found your neck now. How did I forget about that spot at the bottom of your neck where you are so sensitive? Oh, how my tongue loves to glide up from your neck to your ear, softly nipping at it. Are you shivering?

Flip over on your back. Yes, I want to kiss your perfect ass. But I won't stop pleasuring you with my fingers. I want you good and wet for when I slam my hard cock inside of you later. I can feel your pussy swelling from the pressure.

Your clit is there for my taking. I hate to leave your ass, the butterfly kisses I am placing all over it and the tiny licks I place at the bottom that are making you squeal. My mouth wants to taste you.

To have you all over my face as I make you scream with pleasure, and cum with force. Flip back over. I can see your tremendously sexy breasts again. You are so sexy when you're naked. Every curve of your body turns me on.

You like my tongue flickering against your clit? I know you do. You're getting wetter by the Second, and the way your legs are twitching tell me you're close to climaxing. I want my tongue inside of you. My hands are cupping your beautiful breasts, and now I've got your legs bent up.

I can see your delicious pussy. The beautiful contours of it, the lips bright pink and covered in your delicious juices. My tongue loves going in and out of you. Curling up to mimic my cock but releasing when I am inside to lick in circles.

Moan for me baby as I grab your neck. I won't hurt you; just want to hear you gasp with pleasure. Make me know how much you like me touching you as I move my tongue up and down and twirl it between your lips.

You've made my cock so hard I could cum right now on your tits just by looking at you, hot and wet, and ready for me. You can feel my hard cock against your pussy. I'm moving it up and down against it, your wetness, gliding me along as I apply pressure against your clit.

I'm going to fuck you so hard baby, this bed will break. I'm wild just thinking about how good the inside of you is going to feel on my cock. Oh, baby, your pussy is so tight. It fits around my cock like it was made for it. Arch your back so I can move in deeper.

That's right; give me every inch of you to work with. My thrusts are so hard and fast I can barely control myself. The warmth of you is electrifying and my mind is blown away by the sensations pulsing through my body.

Touch yourself for me. I want to see you pleasure yourself while I watch my cock move in and out of your pussy. Your perfect, little tight pussy.

The way your fingers move against your pussy giving you pleasure turns me on so much. I can barely focus on moving my cock in and out of you. But I won't stop. Oh no. I'm going to take you from behind now.

Yes, flip over and get on all fours. You have such an amazing ass. And your back, the contour of it is so sensual. I'm moving slow so I can feel every inch of you more closely. My chest is against your back, the heat from our bodies intermingling. I'm kissing you up and down your spine. Yes, baby, feel me move inside of you, feel your pulse race with my own.

Things are going to move faster now. I cannot wait any longer. I've got you pulled down to the bottom of the bed, I'm standing behind you as you're bent over the edge. I can see your beautiful hair cascading down your sexy back.

I have to pull it, but not too hard. Do you like that? Of course you do. You are in my control, and my cock is now pulsing in and out of you fast and quick. It grows harder with every stroke, wanting to explode inside of you. I want you to cum first. I want to feel your body twitch and have your juices flow all over me.

My fingers have moved to pleasure you while I continue to ram you with my hard cock. Your legs are barely touching the ground, and they are shaking. You can feel the intense pleasure my fingers are giving you against your clit. Shall I flick a little more? I think so.

The combination of my fingers, my cock, and the way your body is responding is so intense.

Cum for me baby, show me just how good I make you feel. That's right, everything is moving so Quick, let go; find your release, as I will find mine.

Yes, I can feel you contracting against my cock. Your back is arching, and you are nearly pulling Away from my cock as the force grows. Don't leave me baby; share your pleasure with me. Let me feel you become fulfilled.

Feel the incredible hardness you have created move deep inside of you; pressing harder with every inch while my fingers create their own pressure. You are so sexy like this, free and close to satisfaction.

One last thrust...one more grip of your breasts from behind, and you cum all over me...

Her Story to Her

"The Soft Satiny Feel Of Your Touch"
Author Jessica Lucas

Your hands are smooth as silk as they glide across my back. Manicured to perfection, each finger a delicate device for pleasure. The touches of your painted red lips are luscious as they trace the area left behind by your hands down the nape of my neck.

We lay naked on the cool sheets.

The chill of the air outside makes its way in from the open window, causing goose bumps to form on our skin and our nipples to grow hard.

It is just nearing the end of winter, when the days are warmer but the evenings are colder than expected. A perfect time to take advantage of lounging in bed, blankets at the ready for when the coolness becomes too much to bear.

With you by my side, staying warm is not a problem. The heat of our bodies, the way we excite one another with a simple touch has kept me warm all winter, and will tonight, as the sky grows darker with each passing minute. I find you irresistible, as you continue to kiss and touch me from behind.

The temptation to pretend I am asleep is great, as I know you will continue caressing every inch of me you can find until I accept your desire.

But I too want to touch you, to glide my hands across your body, smell the almond on your skin; the intoxicating aroma that lingers in every room you have been. I reach my right hand back, remaining on my side, looking away from you.

My hand finds its way to your inner thighs, right between your legs. Not wanting to rush anything along I gently glide the tips of my fingers against you. My nails drawing like an invisible pen on your skin. You take a sharp inhale of breath when my hand accidentally brushes against your sweet spot. I feel the wetness between your legs.

My fingers linger, feeling your warmth, and arousing your body more and more as they play with your softness. I yearn to taste you.

You scoot nearer to me, your breasts pushing up against my back. I can feel their hard firmness against me, and I picture in my mind how beautiful they must look pressing against me.

You have the most amazing breasts. Perfectly shaped like full teardrops, with nipples a soft pale pink that grows hard whenever my tongue is against them. Your leg has made its way up and curls over mine, awaking me from the daydream where your breasts were bouncing up and down as you jumped on the bed atop me, laughing and smiling down at me, completely naked and absolutely captivating.

Then I realize there is no need to daydream because you are here, with me, now.

All I need to do is turn around to face you, nudge my naked body down against yours and I would be able to indulge myself with those perfect breasts. I turn my head to the side and look into your gorgeous face. The long dark eyelashes, round eyes the color of a green valley in spring, and those lips.

Oh, your beautiful plump lips that beg to be kissed. I kiss your hard on the mouth. No tongue, just the pressure of my lips against yours.

I push my backside into you, gently moving my hips back and forth to create friction between our bodies. You grab my breast, squeezing it a tad too hard so I moan while the amazing pain and pleasure sensation runs through my body.

When I break away you greet me with a sly smile, and lick your lips. Oh, how you can turn me

on with just one simple action, one glance at your tongue sends me into a whirlpool of pleasure.
All I have to do is ask. And ask I will.

"I want to feel your tongue on me," I say.

A quick kiss on the lips is your answer, as you crawl up on all fours and I lay on my back, my legs bent up waiting for your approach.

You began by placing tiny kisses on my other lips. The smoothness of your lips, against mine, is delightful. With one long motion of your tongue you touch every inch of me.

I feel you against my sensitive insides, and along the top of my sex. Your tongue sends sensations through me, and when you move your mouth all over me, dancing against me I am overcome with desire.

I watched you on all fours, your head bent down between my legs, ass up in the air.

You could lie down flatter, or even on your side, but you know how much I liked seeing your bottom, the curve of your back, and the tiny waist above slender hips. The way your long, wavy black hair cascades around my thighs turns me on.

The softness of your hair tickles my skin as your head moves. I grab a piece of it in my hand, twirling it between my fingers before gliding it across my stomach. Its soft touch tantalizing, while your tongue works magic on me.

My desire is to feel you against my mouth, my tongue, place my fingers inside of you, and hear the cries of us both moaning in pleasure. I pull tight on your hair, signaling for your head to pop up and look at me. Your eyes, glassy with the clear look of desire, peek at me from below.

Your mouth is wet with my juices, your lips glistening. You smile again, that great big irresistible smile. Without me even having to say a word you climb on top of me, placing your pink velvetiness in my face as you remain on all fours.

I can see every inch of your beauty at this angle. Your toned, long legs on each side, your firm stomach with its adorable crooked belly button, and your breasts hanging down right before my eyes, like two perfectly formed melons about to fall from a tree.

The greatest part of all is the soft spot I am about to feel- it tenses- and gets wetter with every flick of my tongue and snap of a finger.

I take to you voraciously, as if I have been without water for days and need to quench my thirst. My tongue swirls around your clit.

I go inside of you and out again, and even dare to lick you far back; the jolt of a reaction I receive tells me it is an "oh so sensitive" spot.

My tongue having played long enough, I let my fingers have their fun. One finger, then two pressing inside of you; pushing against the warm interior of your body. When three fingers enter you, they fan out and play your body like a piano from the inside, as your mouth comes down on me hard. Your tongue is wild as it slides across me.

You push your hands underneath by ass and grabbing it hard, you lift my pussy up into your face further. The insane pleasure I is feel makes it hard for me to think about anything else, but I need to continue to please you.

My tongue goes back to work as my hands find your breasts. I cup them in my hands, pulling gently and then pushing back. I massage them tenderly, and then pinch your nipples. The accompanying moan tells me you enjoy the pleasure, and the surprised moment of pain.

Your tongue is inside of me now as your face presses against me. I do the same for you, pushing further and further with my mouth as my face is basking in being covered in your wetness.

As if in perfect time with one another, we withdraw our tongues and proceed to swirl with the tips while fingers go in and out and hands grab, tug, and pinch every inch of flesh we find.

Everything starts moving quicker, the room grows a shade darker, and my eyes no longer want to stay open. I arch my back, feeling my climax getting close. Then you take two fingers, press them to the side of each of my lips, and lick with great pressure at the same time. I can hold back no longer. Every part of my body is awakened, and the nectar within me flows out in a great wave of joy.

My climax triggers your own, and I watch your muscles tighten, your pussy flex, feel it grow wetter, until you give in to the moment and expel a great sigh. Your body collapsing onto mine; your arms enfolding my legs as your legs gracefully move to one side.

I lay there, tracing the outlines of your calves with my eyes, the curve of your bottom, and the row of freckles running up your right thigh.

The last image I see is of your sweet smiling eyes before I drift off to sleep knowing that you, this gorgeous creature would be here when I woke up to enjoy again.

~

A Heartfelt Thank You!
To **Everyone** who helped me make RawrWoman.com into a reality.

Our Writers:
Jessica Lucas
Elizabeth Cane
Skyler Knightley
Laney Oden
J.P. George.
Julianna Clemmens
Matt Benson
Derrick Smith
Veronica Fray
Deirdre Wenley
Brooke Jones
Heath Sinclair
Milania Hill
Ingrid Calderon
Sophia Martin
Jacob Summers

Our Voice-Over Team:
Auberon Skye
Regina George
Will B.B.H
Tim L
Andy Love
Jonathan Rider
R.I.
Penelope Canyon
D. Love

Management:
Chris T
Laura L

None of this would be possible without the outstanding teamwork and the passion we all share, Thank You...
P.H.

A Special Thanks To Susan Kelejian,

I have yet to see anyone able to successfully manage multiple tasks at once in high stress environments better than Susan. But more importantly, she does it all with a smile and extremely positive attitude! Susan is intelligent, always willing to help, is a consummate team player, quick on her feet, and is an absolute pleasure to work with. I would wholeheartedly trust in the success of any project or event knowing that Susan was the one seeing it through.

Sincerely,
Peter Hansen.

Publisher/CEO
RawrWoman, Inc.

Contact Information

To find out more about the team behind
RawrWoman.com and to enjoy all our free offerings
please visit: www.RawrWoman.com

Questions? E-Mail: Contact_us@RawrWoman.com

RawrWoman, Inc.
Santa Monica, CA 90403.

When you visit the website, you'll be able to enjoy
all our erotic short stories.

RawrWoman is a collective effort between the erotic
short-story writers, the voiceover artists that bring
the content to auditory life, and the accompanying
pictures we have on display to help walk you
through the story events with some visual stimuli.
We promise you'll never be disappointed with what
RawrWoman offers, and you will always want more.

How do we know our content is outstanding, and
desired by many? One indication occurred a mere
two days after launch, when RawrWoman's traffic
was so large we had to shut down and come back
online with a greater capacity to handle all of our
eager guests.

Erotica for the Soul
Is also available in eBook and audio books.

Immerse yourself into a world of imagination that can take you on a wild ride from having a mysterious stranger take you against your will to a beautiful woman waiting in your bed.

Come. Let's get started...

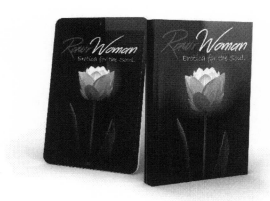